PAGES TORN FROM A TRAVEL JOURNAL

EDWARD LEE

deadite
press

deadite press

DEADITE PRESS
205 NE BRYANT
PORTLAND, OR 97211
www.DEADITEPRESS.com

AN ERASERHEAD PRESS COMPANY
www.ERASERHEADPRESS.com

ISBN: 1-62105-093-9

1 May, 19—
c. 6 p.m.
Somewhere in southeastern Virginia (?)

May Day now, & I feel a cliched & foreboding "prickling of my thumbs," to quote Shakespeare. The irony strikes me with potency–yes, the 1st of May, the Beltane, & the immemorial eve of which so often reflects in my tales: the Druidic and pre-Druidic night of otherworldly phantasmata, the worship of fertility goddesses & celebration of winter's death & the coming spring via orgiastic revel, a time of joyous, lust-ripe fecundity . . .

I'd selected this newer northern-based bus line simply for reduced rates in spite of the more circuitous routes necessitating an extra travel-day. But even with the unexpected $ from Wright, I now fear the delay will prevent my continuing on to New Orleans & its antique granite architecture; its ponderous mausolea & risen burying grounds; its ghost-shrouded swamps; its primal Santerian obsequies; &–most significant–its Vodou-soused atmosphere. Hence, in all probability, my connecting train in Chattanooga would be missed, forcing me to wing a make-shift itinerary. Perhaps next year financial happenstance will license a proper New Orleans tour.

It was through hilly woodland that our course took us since the rail junction in D.C. this morning. The deeper our penetrations, the more degraded the road-paving seemed; but certainly this less-direct route provided the reversal of metropolitan scenery that I preferred. These Virginian hills, however, loomed like immense sentient entities whose various orifi seemed to swallow our coach & plunge us into overgrown darkness. Indeed, the woodland of the U.S. south brings an ambience all its own, differing much from that of my beloved New England. Greens were deeper, the foliage more diverse yet abnormal from overgrowth, & the wooded byways more forebodingly *dark*. Signs of poverty

5

lurked everywhere, tucked away behind flanks of centuried trees & vine-encumbered groves: plank-board houses half-collapsed yet still occupied, pre-'20s motor-vehicles & farm equipment reduced to rusting hulks, primitive shacks & lean-to's populated by families in rotting clothing & malnourished bodies. Twice we spotted Negro corpses hanging from stout limbs, proof that the lynching scourges were ended only by the mouths of prevaricating authorities. Before a sheet-metal shed pocked by cut-out holes for windows, a wax-pallid & filthy-haired adolescent stood cringingly pregnant in mere sackcloth. She appeared to be sucking the innards from the slit belly of a squirrel, her mouth encrimsoned & face flinty. Sunken eyes like those of an octogenarian followed the bus as we passed. I know it was but my imagination, yet those eyes seemed locked on my own. On similar trips I'd seen New England's version of the same despair many times, *nothing* so devastating as this. Whereas New England's woods may well have been ghost-haunted, these of the south stood haunted by the living.

Just as poverty's scars & the over-dense forests grew too oppressive, the bus rumbled out onto a road of better & newer repair, possibly a result of the recent Federal Highway Initiative where workers were paid $1 per day to improve interstate commerce by building more effective roadways. But I sighed as my gaze showed me a sign: RTE. 6, the imperfect number. The vibrations of my karma were already atwitch, even with the refreshing new scenery beyond my window: fields & meadows constellated by all manner of colourful flora. It was at this point, then, there came a suspicious rattling from the rear of the coach where I can only suppose the engine compartment is located. & after that, our dutiful bus driver– did I mention in a previous entry that his eyes seemed watery & unhealthily over-protuberant; while his head appeared more narrow than it should? There was also a peculiarly thick *layering* about the neck that was impossible not to notice. I'll need to use his likeness in an upcoming tale . . .

At any rate, it was this same less-than-gainly driver who made an announcement to the passengers. "Wal haow yew like thet?" rang his dark New England accent. "Engine problems, folks. Saounds like the manifold." (I hadn't a clue as to what a manifold—as a noun–could be. Note: look up.) There were 11 other passengers, & we all moaned in audible unison; yet, wouldn't I know it? 11 plus myself plus the seemingly viced-headed driver equaled 13, the # of ill-omen.

In the name of Nyarlathotep! Though I'm not typically superstitious—a bombast of illogic—the 13 coupled with the 6 & my thumbs' unpleasant tingling did not bode well in my psyche.

But at least better fortune would come in concert w/ the gruelling & likely trip-destroying news. "Thar's a Gawd off-tuh all, ee-yuh!" the driver muttered an exclamation, & was able to wheel the bunglesome coach into a filling station/garage; indeed, when the vehicle stopped, a loud *bang!* erupted from the muffler & the engine sputtered & died.

The garage was a plank-board hovel called, simply, NATE'S GAS & REPAIRS, & boasted a price of 5 cents per gallon for petrol which I believe was 2 cents lower than my northern homestead. My small valise in hand, I stepped out into ambrosial heat after the others debarked (my beloved Providence still possessed an evil chill when I left just days ago, yet even this modest distance more southerly brought a lovely swelter to the air.) The long narrow ribbon of asphalt we'd arrived on seemed to bisect a great field gone wild and heavy, ascending woodland. While the driver conversed w/a grease-smudged mechanic, I & the others straggled into the establishment's poor facsimile for an office; but before entering myself I saw that in either direction, rayed by intense sunlight, nary another building could be seen. I would've liked to know the region's name, yet I hadn't a guess.

Distancing myself from the others (as I am wont to do more times than not) I analyzed my map & deduced that the mechanical mishap had stranded us somewhere in proximity to towns I'd barely heard of, in particular Pulaski & the dubiously named Christiansburg. Very close we must be to the West Virginia as well as the Kentucky border–& a cryptic region notoriously steeped in "white trash" cliches of inbredism &

genetically inherited idiocy, for these same regions were, centuries ago, repositories for England's expelled criminal element. It seems unfair to so negatively brand a region for societal misadventure when in fact the history of *all* regions suffer from it. Grumbling sundry misfortunes, my fellow passengers sat sweat-badged while I remained in leisurely comfort. They were mostly plebeians, I'm sorry to say, & only one man other than myself had retained the dignity to wear a light suit. A pregnant woman, more than likely unwed, sat holding her gravid belly like a bushel basket. She wore Flapperish black bangs, & appeared quite lithe & shapely save, of course, for the grievously swollen stomach; while high & no doubt milk-laden breasts made a visual curio of her. When she asked the time, a surprising cockney accent revealed her British heritage. A gentlewoman she was not, however: her remarkable breasts jutted obviously un-brassiered w/in the threadbare cotton sundress–& when she listlessly parted her legs–gads!!!–the fact that she wore no under-linens disclosed itself. Via her appearance, I believe she was what vulgarians would call a "sauce-box." Several scruffy roughs in their 20's seemed to know each other; their lean, weaselish faces made me think of fugitives; or was that just my naturalistic cynicism bubbling through? The rest were so un-unique in appearance & personality there is no need to distinguish them via words.

Momentarily, the driver came inside w/the proprietor. Nate, the garage's namesake, proved as much by the patch on his begrimed shirt: a short, wiry type, chisel-chinned, w/ biceps like apples. His physical form, facial features, & attire very much bespoke his station in life: a "red-neck" mechanic.

"Ain't the best news for yawl," spake Nate, "and ain't the worst. Yer bus blew the intake manner-fold, and I'se can fix it in a jiff."

"This would be the *good* news, then?" I prompted.

"Yeee-ip. Bad news's that I cain't *get* the blammed gasket till tomorrow mornin'. They'll be drivin' one over from Pulaski."

Another chorus of moans, then someone remarked of the obvious, "So we're stranded here till it's fixed."

"Yeee-ip," replied Nate, hands on hips. The pose displayed the darkened armpits of his work-tunic. "So's yawl can decide fer yerselfs. Ya can spend the night on the bus or"–he shot a thumb in the fashion of a hitchhiker toward road behind him– "hoof it 'bout a mile to Luntville'n flop at the motel. Gilman House, it's called."

Immediately I was enthralled by the divergency of the man's accent. Accents, in fact, has always baited some queer interest in me, with regard to how they mirrored the legacy of the speaker–a societal parallelism; the cruder the accent, i.e., the cruder the man, & the greater the deficit of civility. Our driver, for instance (a Vermonter) carried on his tongue the dialect of a New England jerkwater, a style of speech I was all too familiar with &, I hope, had accurately demonstrated in several tales ("Picture," "Sleep," to name a few). Yet Nate the wiry mechanic cracked in something altogether more unique, what I think of as the accent of the unrefined, poorly educated, low-economic-status Caucasian southerner. All regions had their cultural tongues, & here was a new one on me.

Yet as for the motel–no doubt a discredited fleabag— the prospect I immediately rejected upon being informed of probable $1 ½ per-night fees (outlandish for these economic times and this locale!); while the stubbed-chinned ruffian-trio declined as well, as did the wayward British mother, all clearly as poor if not poorer than I. In my time I'd slept on many a bus to save much filthy lucre. Best to be prudent regarding creature comfort, & keep more funds available for some indulgence. The others deputed at once, to retrieve bags & baggage from the coach luggage compartment, & begin the simple trek on foot. (I did however like the *name* of the motel– the Gilman House. It had a nice creepish ring to it. I'll have to use it in an upcoming tale, along with the suspicious likeness of the driver.)

A simple query of "Nate" afforded me directions to the commode facilities (the "donniker," he called it), & upon entrance to the cubby I was slammed in the face by an absolutely miasmal urine/excreta odor so common amongst these out-of-the-way stops. Yet holding my breath, nearly teary-eyed by the vaporous stench, I proceeded to my business into a toilet *horrific* beyond description–an observation of some peculiarity for a travelogue, yet write it I remain inclined. Here, indeed, a 2nd auspex occurred, a premonition of cogent effect. My thumbs did tingle as the unknown divination heightened, for amid typical crude scrawls of telephone #'s & names promising all manner of sexual formidability, my eyes stopped on a single graffito revealed via the crudest stick-figure drawing: a grinning male figure with obvious erection. Lying elevated before him was a stick-figure woman, arms & legs asprawl, circles for breasts & dots for nipples, a clump of pen-squiggles for private hair, then bugged eyes & a jutting tongue. It was the simplicity of the grotesqueness that had snagged my eye, not art-work at all, but an appallingly demented representation of a deranged mind. See, at first glance, the actions of the 2 stick-figures remained paradoxical, but as I scrutinized details . . .

The male, clearly, was inserting his erection *into the crown of the prone female's head* . . .

What madness was this to so visually vandalize the chamber's wall, & what manner of *pervert* had drawn it? The speculation was as depressing as it was beguiling. Indeed, who could even *think* of so depraved a thing?

Darkness, then, seemed to settle over my soul.

The world was changing ever-so-grimly, it seemed. A trifling matter–just a crude scrawl by a demented hand–yet for reasons I could not reckon with, I felt as though a portent had been infused into my very psychic fiber.

Before I quitted the abysmal closet, I penned a graffito of my own: *cthulhu fhtagn.* Still, the ignorant drawing left me imbued in despair. I tried to recompose myself when I went back to the front office, loosening my neck tie & removing my jacket. At this point I was informed that the 3 scruffs had lit off for a nearby lake with their fishing rods that they'd unsecured from the coach's luggage hold; presumably the pregnant Briton had joined them, to allay boredom. Other riders were already departing for the short walk to lodgings. "Gentlemen," I spake to Nate & the bus operator, "if you'll excuse me, I believe

10

I'll take advantage of these lush Virginian surroundings for a nature walk."

Nate grinned wickedly at my notice, & said, "Sometimes there's creeker gals swimmin' in the lake–buck naked, they'll be," er—at least that's what I *think* he said, the word "creeker," yet he'd pronounced it more as "cricker," which I presumed to be a hill-dweller of an even more rustic bent than Nate. "If'n yer lucky, you'll get to gander some"–he rubbed his hands together as if greedy–"and, yee-ip, I ain't kiddin' ya, a lotta them backwoods hosebags are *lookers*. Got big ole tits settin' out like Thanksgivin' supper, yes sir!"

"Thet sew?" asked the driver in his own conflicting accent.

"Dang straight, buddy. And pussies? Shee-it! They got big hairy pussies just *drippin'* to get poked, and I'se mean drippin' like a blammed *honey jar* turnt upside-down! And sometimes you'll a-see 'em ettin' each other, no lie." He winked right at me. "Like to make ya wanna jerk out a creamer."

This outrageous excess of information & crudity left me staring, but even more regrettably, Nate continued as if in a *fever* of vulgarness, still rubbing his hands together, "Yee-ip, I'll tell ya, man. *Some* 'a them hill girls out there're so sick in the head for dick, you'll shit your ever-livin' *pants!*"

I nearly gasped.

The bus driver piped in, "Sick in the head fer dick, yew say? Yew know, up narth we got gulls like thet tew, like they juss curn't get *enough* of it. Way a rummy needs rum? These gulls need *dick* stuck in 'em, ee-yuh."

"Aw, shore, girls like that ever-where, man," Nate replied. "S'way they was made, yessir! Was made ta be *filled* with cum, and fer ever minute goes by that they ain't, it's a blammed cryin' shame. A bunch'a *fuck-pots* is what they is, an' IIIIIIIIIII'se love 'em!"

The driver laughed. "'I heer thet, feller!"

"But mind ya, these creeker tramps? The ones deeper in the hills, they'll try ta charge ya money but if'n ya ain't got none, they'll likely fuck or suck ya anyway. That's how dag blammed *horny* they is. Dick in the mouth or dick in the kitty, either way they *gots* ta have it . . . "

11

Paling, I uttered, "I . . . appreciate being so apprized," as I could stand *not one moment more* of Nate's butchery of the English language & dizzying entreatment of profane exposition, but then as I hastened outside, Nate crackled laughter along with the slab-necked bus driver.

Gads! What a thing to experience! The human sexual condition never fails to astound me. While I had *no* desire to behold "backwoods hosebags" "ettin'" each other, I did need a walk to clear my head of its sudden & inexplicable sense of foreboding along with the recent backwash of psychic detritus. Yet Nate's crudities served to reinforce the dark truth I'd only started to learn in New York: that too much of the world revolved around matters of base & morbid carnality. Now removed from the squat repair building, I embarked into blazing sun & the sights of sweeping fields to the north & dense-packed woods to the south. Across the narrow asphalt ribbon, I spied the pregnant one waddling cumbersomely into a trail posted with a makeshift sign that read simply LAKE with a painted arrow pointing. Presumably she meant to join the rube fishers. So distended was her belly that she braced it as she walked w/interlocked fingers beneath its considerable girth. She stopped, glanced once over her shoulder at me, then continued & disappeared into the overgrown trail.

The weather could not have been more propitious, and I found a trail proceeding in the opposite direction & at once let myself be engulfed by it. The woods off the road were redolent w/delightful fresh spring smells, and locusts trilled pleasantly. Scenic strolls, just like scenic bus & train rides, were welcome opportunities for the esthete in me to emancipate my mind of life's discord & to ponder upcoming tales. But after the queer observation in the commode—& Nate's harrowing dissertation of local female proclivities—I found creative concentration beyond the realm of the possible.

Nate's endorsement of the "creekers" stuck to me like a gadfly. Certainly some women, just as some men, were possessed of accelerated sexual yearnings, perhaps forged by upbringing or environment, or some hormonal imbalance as certain recent scientific journals were known to imply, though

I was hardly the expert. I can only speak of my own libido which has always seemed to run on the low side. In times past, when the endless discourse with my New York Group turned to matters of crudity, it was made known to me that certain women exist stricken with syndromes such as *nymphomania* & *erotopathia*–hmm. Sonia, during my short-lived term of wedlock, had gone through such spates, for sure. She'd wake me from a sound sleep as though I were a vender on demand! & once Little Belknap, in one of his coarser turns of talk, had referred to a species of woman "hell-bent for cock," he'd said; & CAS–quite the ladies man–had made similar references in his wild missives: women *obsessed* with the male privates. If I remember with any accuracy, he'd called them "head-queens," of all things. I'd scoffed at such talk but then I was admittedly *not* an authority. For amusement I tried to think of a more scholarly appellation—a sufferer from some acute *pudendamaniacal* syndrome. Indeed, a *genitalus obsessus!*

Truly I am the odd man out in this world of musky lasciviousness–I find most of human nature deplorable & most of the human species cretin-like, *people* akin to the filling station itself: *human* hovels; while my cohorts jokingly dub me the misanthrope. I can only hark back to my short tale of the necropolis. I am an outsider.

Yet an outsider with some pomp. While many men would join in to the gutter-talk as a means of demonstrating masculinity, I know that it was my culture, my superior breeding & gentry that were the admixture which triggered my revulsion. But now, however, I'd be dishonest to refute . . .

Something about Nate's foul-mouthed rant left me . . . sexually enlivened.

My privates verifiably throbbed.

I let my mind wander as I traversed the sedate trail, shaded by branches of century-old trees. Amid quotidian shelf-fungus, tree boles, flowery vines, one out-of-sort discovery stopped me in my tracks:

A yellowed mammalian skull–most probably canine–with a hole in it.

Later

In correspondence, August once referred to an associate who'd undertaken side-employment as a seller of lightning rods. This occurs to me now only as an undue *abstraction,* for I myself feel akin to a lightning rod, not one that attracts nature's storm-born electrical emissions but instead?

Human sexual perversity.

With each step of my walk, it seemed, thoughts overtly sexual rankled me & filled my head with the most obscene images, i.e., Nate's creekers, "sick in the head for d—." Did such creatures genuinely exist? Thus far, I had seen none, & the more decent side of my reason hoped that the indelicate mechanic's promises were pure invention. But . . . what of my *less*-than-decent side?

& all the while, that bathroom graffito left me helpless but to ponder what it insinuated. Such thoughts never occurred to me; they were useless thoughts, they were a waste of my precious faculties & shameful to be entertained by someone of erudite persuasions such as myself. I'd walked perhaps a mile down the trail, until it grew impassable; whereupon I retraced my steps, but after an undue amount of time I realized, 1), that the nature walk had indeed, finally, purged me of those obsessive sexual images which so distracted me, &, 2), I'd over-bound my starting point. Where was the exit spur back to the main highway &, further, the garage?

It was now that my "lightning-rod" analogy socked home. I heard–or *thought* I heard—a sound like the tiniest squeal whose tenor did not let on whether it be a squeal of panic or a squeal of delight.

Through some bushes, then, I thrust my head.

Like a great glimmering mirror, a small lake shined back at me–of course, Nate had mentioned a lake close by, hadn't he? To wither the 3 roughs had repaired for a bout of fishing. However, when my gaze circumscribed the modest body of water, it revealed no signs of the men themselves, though 3

14

fishing rods were indeed apparent, each with its haft stuck in the ground at the shoreline.

Then it was the squeal that came to my ears again, & then? Another more deliberate sound.

Crack!

Yes, a hard, wet smack, quite akin to a palm hauled across the cheek in violence. Behind a sprawl of unruly bushes I rose on tiptoes to afford a view—

& stood in utter shock.

There, several yards off the lake's edge, I beheld a most primal congregation: the 3 surly roughs on their knees in the dirt, & whom they all knelt about was the huge-bellied Brit mother. All 4 of them were naked as proverbial jay birds.

The woman lay squirming, her knees painfully jacked back nearly to her shoulders as one of the lean rubes fornicated with her so vigorously it could only be described as savage. Her breasts & belly jolted with each pelvic thrust. "Oh, I'll get another 'un off in ya, I will," grunted the man.

It boggled my mind to see such ferocious intercourse with a woman so close to term; yet it was the other 2 ruffians who disturbed me all the more. One leaned over, & there could be no mistake that he was *biting* the woman's left nipple, after which she cringed & shrieked. & the other?

crack!

It was this 3rd rube who laid his open palm hard across her cheek.

Clear to me then it was–in my investigatory nature-stroll– that I'd stumbled upon an overt rape & beating; & while I am not a man made for imbroglio—

crack! crack! crack!

–I knew that I must come at once to this woman's defense, & with only my meager fists & barely existent muscles as weapons. But as I made to do exactly that, knowing well that I'd be thrashed to a spindly pulp, the most shocking truth of all unveiled itself.

After the most recent crack across the face, the woman inclined up with a fuming frown, & her accent rang: "What is it with you yanks, anyway? When I say bite me, I mean no less!" & then she glowered at the fornicator, who'd stopped mid-thrust–"and can't you fuck a bird's minge harder than *that?*"

The man's naked chest gleamed in sweat, while his face crumpled in perplexion. "Well, dang, we each done put two in ya already! I'se humpin' hard as I can!"

"Well hump *harder,* love, like you *mean* it," she griped, & then, to the 3rd: "And if American blokes can't slap a *woman* with any more spunk than what you're doing, how'd you managed to whip us in two wars?"

So yet again, the cosmic laugh was on *me.*

The perverse woman's complaints seemed to cense her 3 suitors. Now the brute copulation recommenced w/a vengeance, such that I feared her fetal water would be untimely summoned. Several minutes ensued as such, & next the man's face twisted into a rictus of the most basal disdain; & he extracted himself, stood up, & slaked himself of hand, dropping lines of seminal slime onto the woman's quivering belly. "Yeah, man!" railed one of the others. "Shine the limey bitch *up!*" but his accent, which I'd been thus far unable to place, pronounced the "shine" as *shan.* When the emission abated, its depositor crudely rubbed those same procreative wares all about the woman's great belly, leaving her intensely agleam. Then he guttered, "Bitch wants ta get fucked hard, huh? Well, *I'll* show her hard," & as the other 2 continued to alternately bite & slap, he trotted off naked only to return in a moment . . .

With one of the fishing rods.

Dark cackles circled about the obscene spectacle. "Yeah, stick it *to* her, Corey!" one egged on. When the woman herself saw what was about to be inserted into her, it was not horror she reacted with, it was *encouragement!* She moved her frantic hands to her bared privates, using her fingers to widen the aperture & assist the unnatural invasion.

Hoots, hollers, & whistles ensued evilly as the fishing-rod's stout haft sunk into the woman's private egress; then the effort of its bearer produced a long, slow piston effect. It was the outrage of all outrages, an ultimate sickness-induced

exploitation of nature. All the while came the woman's wanton pant; her face grew puff-eyed, & her salacious grin sharpened to the point of drooling. In & out proceeded the obscene rod-handle. The chuckles rose, & when one bit down again on a gorged nipple, the woman's back arched with a convulsant abruptitude, & from her throat burst a propulsive scream of such pitch, I broke out into gooseflesh. Lastly–
CRACK!
–her final demand was discharged as the next slap across her face knocked her to undisputable dizziness & rolled her eyes back in her head; after which she began to shiver seizure-like as her climax was finally achieved.

The final withdrawal of the rod-handle proved it had reached a depth of a foot, somehow without rupturing the intricacies of the woman's womb. Moments later, the men collapsed, wither-penised & exhausted; yet the woman hopped up almost cheerily & bid in the shining accent, "Thanks, fellas! The fucking most Yanks manage ain't worth a bag of wank and a brown trout, but that was fair to midland–now I think I'll have a dip," & with this, she waddled off–nude & enthused–toward the lake, as if nothing untoward had taken place.

Dusk

My disheartenment stalked me for the remnant of daylight's hours. Blast the Fates for throwing such raving *lewdness* across my otherwise meek-minded path. What I'd seen heretofore seemed to provoke a deep self-rumination. Certainly, the weird tales I'd spent my adulthood crafting were *rife* with implied procreative aberrancy; why witnessing it in reality's scape should disjoint me so, I could not estimate. Was I, in my wee tales, venting speculations–or even phantasies–otherwise kept reticent in my subconscious? This I shuddered to contemplate.

& I shuddered further to realize something I would never admit to a living soul: the sexual *unnaturalness* I'd watched take place on that lake shore left me decidedly & ashamedly aroused, more so even than before.

A man of breeding & civility should *not* feel this way, yet I did all the same. This strange trip was growing stranger & stranger, as though we'd broken down on some forbidden access between the stream of the normal world & some other half-real macrocosm of deviant ravenings & staggering lust. August would brand such harrowing departures from generative normalcy as the by-product of a society losing sight of God; but as an atheist I see it only as a rising signalisation of the times. It is concrete & unanimous *morality* that breeds order & culture, not the fear of the wrath of August's deity. (& should I be in error? That same God will damn me to eternal torment, no doubt complete with pitchfork-wielding daemons & smoking labyrinths of brimstone!) Nevertheless, my quandaries are enough to solicit the devil; yet I do not believe in *him*, either.

I frittered time in the office as the sun westered, while Nate worked on smaller jobs in the garage bay. Via small-talk w/the bus operator, I came to learn that the 3 "roughs" were brothers, venturing south back to their home somewhere in Florida, while nothing was known of the Brit. I jotted out

18

some postcards, then worked on this travelogue till the small, drear-paned windows began to tinge with darkness. Sometime later, the pregnant Briton drifted in & made the strangest comment: "There's something in the air tonight, eh?"

Apparently I'd begun to drowse. The gravid woman appeared blurred, while her features of fecundity (i.e., her breasts, her curvatures, & of course the life-gorged abdomen) appeared exaggerated as of a cartoon. "Pardon?" I mumbled.

Her face beamed, though her eyes looked flat, & in grainy half-light she turned to a small window to peer out, seeming to see more than was there. Her English accent sounded sputtery, like a suet-candle. "Sometimes the way the stars are . . . It's Fate *choosing* us."

The bizarre words roused me. "Whatever do you mean, Miss?"

"Oh, you know, Mister. Seems its chosen *you* today. Like a radio antenna, hmm?"

"Or lightning rod?" I croaked without forethought.

She turned, grinned right at me, & nodded, but then ever-so-slowly the grin turned devilish. "Those three blokes– they're still sodding about at the lake, fishing. I'm gonna go *fuck* 'em all again for a free fish dinner–that is, if their Yankee Hamptons got anything left to give up. Hope that previous fucking hasn't left 'em too airy-fairy for another go."

I gulped at the comment.

"A bird's gotta do what she's gotta do in these bad times, eh? What with ackers bein' rare as rocking-horse shit," & then she giggled in a sound like a drove of rodents.

The moment's strangeness filled my head with a drone. Her pose drew my gaze such that a part of me grew frightened, as though the spirit of some *other* had transmigrated itself into the vessel of her flesh. My stare locked me in rigor as she brazenly smoothed her hands up the corpulent belly, then caressed her bosom; & after a moment of this she actually lifted her sundress up over the breasts to reveal all to my eyes. Yet it was the grin above all that nailed me to my chair.

"It chooses me a lot"–her words seemed to cluck–"but tonight it's definitely chosen you." The fingers of one hand twisted a nipple substantial as a baby's pacifier; her other hand played with deliberation amid the fur between her legs.

I squirmed. "Really, Miss–you're causing me quite a bit of discomfort . . . "

"Oh, I'm sure I am, love. Taken quite a fancy ta me Bristols, proves you ain't an arse-bandit," and then she laughed. "I saw you today–hiding behind that bush at the lake. You were havin' quite a look, weren't ya?"

With instantaneousness, my face reddened.

"Aw, yeah, dearie, I saw you watchin' them three gutterscums fuckin' me ta hell and back, and stickin' that pole up me minge, and you *fancied* what you were seein', didn't you?"

For the life of me I could not respond, & I can only hope that her entire hand did not *really* disappear into her sex. No, it was merely my imagination, jaded by the queerness of the moment . . .

She ceased the self-molestation, then righted her worn gown. Did her great, tight belly quiver as I watched? It was to something as faintly audible as the wind that her words now reduced themselves to. "You should've joined in–I hoped you would," she said, turning her back to me to re-stare out the dim window. "You're a high and might one, you are. Oh, yes, a real sophisto. But you'll be wanking later thinking of me. And if you think banging the daylights out of a pregnant bird is twisted . . . just wait till tonight . . . "

In spite of the warmth, I shuddered at a clear chill. "Tonight?" my tone begged.

But she'd already quitted the seedy office & was out the door & crossing the road to the lake trail.

My God.

Had she been touched by some premonitory insight? She'd spoken as though something grim remained in store for me, & as for her actions? I felt disgusted with my uncomfortable yet undeniable arousal.

How eccentric it is: this organic machine called the human brain whose neurotransmitters & hormonal brew keep the host at odds with himself. No, the night was too weird, nauseously so. I thought then of De Quincey's helpless chasing of the "dragon," for it was through the veil of that narcotic that surely he pondered some other world of hyper-reality which served as the fodder for his art; & Poe, too, via the fermented spirits which bid his beggarly demise but whose stupors showed him his true Muse which lives forever while he himself has degraded to dust. Where did that leave me, then? Mordant, querulous, a hypocritical bigot–yes. I couldn't have felt more empty just then. The yearning of my groin strained, begetting more shame & self-disgust. For distraction, I looked out the window. No sign could be found of the gravid tart; no doubt she'd returned to her ruffian suitors to slake more primal needs. Whereas in daylight, the woods had looked vibrant & plush, now they appeared primeval, overgrown & hauntedly twisted. Twilight flickerings through darkness of more onerous depth seemed impossibly to settle about the drab wooden building. I nearly yelped at a sudden clatter behind me. A light flicked on.

"No need to sit in the dang dark," the mechanic, Nate, chuckled. He gained entry through an ancillary door.

"Oh, you startled me," I stumbled.

The man cracked the top off a pop bottle. "What'cha always writin' in that book? You a writer?"

"I simply keep a journal of my travels," I replied, having long-since learned never to reveal my imponderable profession. "It seems late," I observed, "but it's not really. Only eightish."

He flapped a hand. "Aw, what's time anyway? Usually takes too long ta go by, ya ask me. Sure as shit wish there was sumpthin' ta *do* tonight."

The profanity vexed me. "A good book is always a means to boredom's end," I said. "Have you ever read–"

"Aw, I mean sumpthin' fun–but who's got money fer *that,* huh?" & then he cracked a boisterous laugh, though I found absolutely no comedic merit in what he'd said. Then, however, & nearly in unison, we both stiffened at the sound of a long wooden creak as of a heavy foot on the porch outside. I fancied I saw a tall shadow begin to bend like a fevered hallucination. Was something silhouetted by moonlight standing just outside

21

the screen door? Nate exclaimed under his breath, "Jumpin' Jesus, who the hell's–"

It was a figure nearly doubled over who stepped silently into our midst: a man in clothes like tent canvas & wearing, of all things, a bellman's cap. He'd entered bent-over due to a shocking abnormality of physical height; even inside now, he was unable to stand upright. No doubt existed that he must be at least over 7 feet tall.

Beady, overly round eyes seemed to squint in a head that seemed too small, almost shrunken. It was Nate those eyes addressed. "Good even-time, Sar. I beg only absolution for any intrusion I might be encumbering thee with," he spake in the strangest antique diction. "Mightn't I be enquiring of ye proprietor?"

Nate scratched his head at the sight of great stooped man. "I run the joint if'n that's what ya mean and–holy *hail*, buddy! Ain't never seen no one tall as you in my life!"

"So much more than I, good Sar, thee have never before seen, ye spectacles most incredulous." The man had several paper tubes tucked under his arm; & one of them he unrolled with a single flap of an enormous hand. "I beg thy permission to post this notice in thy window–in exchange, mind thee, for admission at no cost to thee."

It was a poster of the most intricate illustration, entitled along the top:

O'SLAUGHNASSEY'S TRAVELLING SHOW!
RIDES!
CONCESSIONS!
ODDITIES OF NATURE!
THRILLS FOR THE WHOLE FAMILY!
COME ONE, COME ALL!

"Well tickle my stick, a carnival!" enthused Nate. "That the same one was here last year?"

"Indeed, Sar, the same."

"I never got chance to make it on account'a work but a couple'a chums tolt me it was a doozy! S'you'll give me free tickets to hang that in my wind-er?"

The tall man nodded awesomely & passed the mechanic a cutting of tickets. "Thy fine graces are bountied in the most, good Sar, and I shan't scruple to detain thee any farther of thy goodly nature. Thee may trust in my word as a gentleman of verity that *O'Slaughnassey's* Travelling Show be ye finest, ye most complete, and more striking than any thee might ever have conceived," & then the man hung the poster so to show its front out the window. Nate & I went outside with him, where he now was able to stand without hindrance. Truly he was a natural giant, & more so in other regards as, first, I caught Nate casting a brief, frowning glance at the titan's crotch, after which my own eyes followed suit reflexively. He shook each of our hands, his own being double the length & breadth of mine, & offered, "Gentlemen, I am distinguished to have been led into thy midst, and look with much anticipation to seeing thee at the show . . . "

My distraction took moments to fend off, for, you see, the crotch of the man's trousers appeared quite disproportionately *stuffed.*

He walked off in leviathan strides, collapsed himself into a waiting spoke-wheeled truck, & drove away.

"Ain't that a kick?" Nate remarked, hands ever on his hips. "Looks like we got sumpthin' fun ta do after all."

"Fortunateness seems to have granted your wish," I said, eyeing the poster.

"Shit-yeah'n a great big *fuck* ta boot!"

I frowned.

Mussed-haired from an apparent nap, the bus driver appeared, & thus began Nate's indelicate dissertation regarding the show & cost-free admission tickets. "Haow yew like thet! A curnervul!" enthused the driver. "En't ben tew one in yeers . . . "

"Nor have I," I contributed, recalling similar travelling shows that would come to the Stamper Hill region periodically. More times than not, however, I could not attend due to the ubiquitous writer's curse–i.e., I didn't have the *money!*

Nate sharpened his perpetually snide grin. "Friend'a mine tolt me 'bout this one last year, & said they had a crew'a carny whores ta *die* fer!"

"Ee-yuh, I believe it," said the driver. "I went me to a curnervul in Brattleboro onct, and the hoo-ers theer drained me dry. Ee-yuh, suh. If spunk was garbage, theer pussies'd be a dumpin' grounds. Ask me, theer en't a better place for a feller to send his jism than up a curny hoo-er's cooch."

"Or up her tailpipe!"

"Er in her gut, for thet matter!"

"Or–hail! All three!"

I felt dissolute. The level of vocal vulgarity & overall vitiated moralism staggered me in place; though being the stranger in strange company I struggled to maintain some demeanour. Only when the driver saw fit to slap me on the back, did I actually blanch.

"En't that right, Slim?" he gruffed, laughing. "You ever git'cher peter-snot up in a carny whore's cunt?"

Stupefied, I could only falteringly reply, "I'm sad to say that I have never had the benefit of the experience . . . "

"But ya'd lak to, wouldn't ya?" Nate asked with some concern.

As for the opportunity of conveying my "peter-snot" into such a creature, I wanted to answer that the notion of my caring less was most definitely an issue of total impossibility. Being the sport, however, I replied, "Why, of course . . . "

The mechanic rocked back & forth on his heels. "Well tonight's yer lucky night, 'cos we'll be a-goin'. That tall feller gave me three tickets–one fer each'a us."

The driver erupted a hoot. "And I thurt it'd be a dullard's night!"

"We'se havin' us some *fun!*" & with *this* exclamation, Nate performed a vocal demonstration that I believe is referred to as a "rebel-yell."

I raised a querying finger. "I believe you aforementioned something about an associate of yours endorsing this show last year?"

"Aw, shee-it yeah, man!" Nate's eyes gleamed vulpurine at the tickets. "An', see, this friend'a mine? Dolman Nale's his name–he runs couple'a stills up in the woods, but it was Dolman tolt me 'bout this self-same carnival last year'n how dandy the whores turned out, but see, what he couldn't quit ravin' 'bout was this one whore in *particular* . . . "

The driver's interest was duly piqued. Mine, however, was not.

"Said they had this li'l blondie whore with a smile could launch a thousand ships and a rack'a tits like to make a monsignor pull his hair out–"

The driver *roared* laughter.

Nate's seedy grin inclined toward us. "But ya know what else?"

"Whut?" pleaded the driver.

"I daren't contemplate," came some veiled sarcasm from me.

Nate's voice fell to a whisper. "She has hands for feet . . . "

The driver's already odd face transformed to something odder in reaction to Nate's cryptic words. "I curn't be heerin' yew right. Yew say hands for–"

"I say she gots *hands* where her blammed *feet* should be!"

"No!"

"'S'a fact. Dolman Nale ain't one fer tall tales."

Though my own faith in this Mr. Nale's credulity fell pointedly short of Nate's, I had heard of similar anomalies– *chromosomal,* evidently, based on the fascinating research of Johannsen & Mendel of years ago. The theory is thus: that once an ovum is positively fertilised, discrete constituents called "gene-markers" are mysteriously activated. The resulting embryo-genesis ensues; however, *flawed* gene-markers may, for a myriad of reasons, come into play, triggering abnormal development.

"Yee-ip, I ain't kiddin' yawl. Gal was born with hands fer feet–and born without teeth too–"

"No teeth, nuther?" said the driver.

"Not a chopper in her yap, no sir!" Nate gave a lewdly knowing nod. "But it's on account'a that that she sucks the best pecker in the land. Dolman Nale, he's *had* some dick-suckin' in his time, but he says she's the *best,* and don't charge much neither. Says the gal also does a show–"

The driver crossed his arms. "A shew, yew say?"

"Yee-ip. They got a bunch'a peep-tents there, they call 'em. For, like, ten cents worth'a tickets, you can look in and watch."

The words unwittingly goaded a question I could not repress. "Watch *what?*"

"Watch the whores gettin' poked by stunt-cocks—you know."

"I assure you–I *don't* know. Stunt—"

He dramatically grabbed his crotch & hefted it. "They'se carnies with really big dicks."

"Ee-yuh," augmented the driver. "An' for fellers who en't got the dough for a hoo-er, he curn at leest watch'n have at himself with his hand."

"Oh," I muttered.

"Yee-ip," Nate aggravatedly repeated. "And this blondie, this gal with hands for feet? What she do in her tent is she beats off four fellas at once. Get it?"

First the deduction, then the horrendous picture, formed in my mind. "Ah, I see . . . "

"And like I said, the fellas is all packin' really big cocks, and what they do, see, is they all slap down their jizz on her, for what they'se call the *wet*-shot. Shee-it, Dolman tolt me that poor gal looked like a dang *rum bun* time them stunt cocks was done a-cummin'."

The driver percolated laughter.

My element, surely, this was not, but I stood determined to go along since Nate's inference that a free ticket had my name on it. My only interest was the change of scenery & possibly–should finances allow–a candied apple. I'd leave the "peep-tents," & the "hoo-ers," to them.

Nate cracked his hands together like a pistol shot. "Well, hail. What're we'se waitin' for, boys? It ain't far, and I'se got my truck."

"I'm much obliged to be included," I told him.

"Ee-yuh," added the driver for the nth time, &–for goodness sake, he rubbed his crotch! "I need ta fuck me a hoo-er in the wuss way."

Nate fumbled for keys in his pocket. "I just hope that blondie with hands for feet is there this year."

A moment previously, my eyes found their way back to the poster advertisement. "If this hanging is timely, I'd say you're in luck."

Both men drifted over as my finger directed their attention. The poster turned out to be an elaborate artistic endeavor &, in specificity, a helix of detailed sketch-illustrations which furnished an eye-catching border for the sensational lettering. I'll add that the artist demonstrated a talent akin to a hybridization of Dore & Brundage: evocative & if anything *too*-detailed representations of the carnival's repertoire of personnel. It was here that I became engrossed, as did my associates. It was a rich & grotesque tableau that formed the poster's curtilage, commencing, first, typically: the Bearded Lady; the Mermaid of Ponape; the World's Oldest Man, the Sword Swallower; the 500-Pound Woman; an interspersion of double-headed livestock & an Oddities Room proffering jars of variously anomalous fetuses; then, far more attention-arresting: a cadaverous, sunk-eyed female (Cadaveressa, Revived From the Clutches of Death By African Magic!), an impish little girl (The 45-Year-Old Child!), a ghostly 3-eyed man (The Tri-Clops!), &, at the bottom, the target of my notice: Bliss! The Girl with Hands for Feet!

It was this drawing that the 3 of us scrutinized.

The tiny yet intricate oddment of art depicted a robustly bosomed young woman sitting spraddled & smiling brightly through a most beatific & even angelic visage; arms extended as well as legs, the latter sporting hands where nature would ordinarily attach feet.

"Dang if that ain't her!" Nate cried out.

"Juss like yew're buddy said," added the moronic driver.

All a likely story, I presumed. The majority of such outlandish carnival exhibits would turn out, after more scrutinous review, to be rife with fraud &, hence, bait for the gullible. But what did I care? A few hours of distraction would surely benefit my mood, & the ticket was any writer's favorite price.

The passage of a few minutes found us on our way. The means of our transport? Nate's dent-ridden & rust-patched rattletrap of a truck, which endeavored noisily along the road that wound about the darkening woodline. The vehicle's inferior suspension brought a frown to my lips over each bump, while further frowns were elicited due to my 2 unpolished companions, both of whose body odor raged, not to mention incessant discourse replete with language the likes of which might urge the lowliest of gargoyles to become sickened to the point of projectile emesis. Simple decency demands that I repeat no excerpts in this humble travelogue.

Dusk brought the day's quiescence, slowly draining vivid darkness into the quaint rural scenes ahead. I chuckled as a duo of bats glided crazily across our passage, for Nate & the driver curtailed their coarse talk momentarily as if the tiny black *chiropterans* foreran doom. Of other motorists/pedestrians on the road, we encountered none, though the trek did clatter us past a handful of decrepit, wood-slat domiciles complete with "hayseeds" sitting in front-porch rocking chairs; as well as a badly white-washed general store & a feed & fertilizer supplier, all tucked oddly off the road & half-into overhanging woods as if shunning something. When we rounded the next bend, however, the forest abruptly gave way to an expanse of great open space that I'd estimate being a mile square. "This here's Tuckton's Fields," Nate explained. "Ain't nothin' but dirt-scratch land on account'a the soil got wored out after the War'a Northern Aggression."

I thought it gentlemanly *not* to point out that said conflict was actuated by *Southern* aggression, my being a "Yankee" as far as his concern went. "Presumably via the failure of sufficient crop-rotation cycles," I offered. "Had they rotated between cotton and soya, the soil would still possess vitality."

Nate made a confused smirk. "They throw the county fair here, too, and some other hootenannies'n things," the noun in terminus being articulated as "thangs."

I'm fairly certain that the bus driver, as he inclined forward to squint at the vast tract of land, rubbed his crotch. "I en't seein' me no curnervul heer, feller " but just then, the remaining edge of woodline broke to show us a dusk-tinged panorama whose epicenter existed as a virtual *efflorescence* of multicoloured light. It seemed that a colossal living fireball throbbed amid the barren field.

"There it 'tis, buddy!" Nate wailed. "The whores are a-waitin'!"

"Eeeeeeeeeeeeeeeeee-YUH!" added the driver. "Ee-yuh, ee-yuh, ee-yuh, ee-yuh, ee-yuh, ee-yuh!"

Seven–that's right–*seven* "ee-yuhs!" I could not have sighed with more decisive despondency.

A single rutted road bisected the expansive field, a linearly perfect lane leading directly to this blossom of illumination. Closer, the blossom queerly increased in size, & gave up details previously diffused by distance: spiring towers with blinking pinnacles, garlands of flashing orbs, a gargantuan ferris wheel turning like a landed star; an aura glowed about the entire goliath of activity–and sound as well, gun-fire-like laughter, gleeful screams in the wake of soaring roller coasters, & colliding, gladsome melodies from a plentitude of pipe organs. The awesome sight carried with it the very acme of festiveness.

My own awe widened my eyes as our approach slowed; truly, the carnival stretched immense, claiming dozens of acres. Nate stopped the truck in a common area awry with all-manner of motors; and after properly parking, we were off.

I nearly shuddered from the sheer *immensity* of the enterprise. At the entrance–a wooden archway painted with scenes of frivolity–we stood in a lengthy line; I used this time to look up at the dizzying erections of rails, girders, tracks, & coruscating lights to realize that this travelling show tinied the few my past had shown me. Its border was formed by the show's transport trucks & personnel trailers, every 10 yards or so by large, cross-armed ruffians in meretricious garb, functioning as sentinels to insure that none infiltrate the carnival without rendering payment. While in wait, I contemplated the incalculable *toil* of an effort such as this: the sheer manpower of transport, the logistics, disassembling & then erecting all of *this;* it occurred to me, too, how *unqualified* I would be in a such a troupe.

Soon that painted archway admitted us maw-like, whereupon Nate provided our tickets, & it was a happy pandemonium into which we were then disgorged. "Why not we look fer them whores lickety-split, don't'cha think?" Nate's reprobate question turned more of the wonderful English language into carnage.

The bus driver replied with enthusiastic, "Ee-YUH!" & once again rubbed his crotch.

"'Specially that purdy blondie with hands fer feet'n no teeth. Can you *imagine* the suck-job she kin lay on us?"

"I believe I'll embark first on a reconnoiter of my own," I explained, "for surely in my inexperience, my tagging along would present a burden to your own motives. We'll meet up shortly–"

The bus driver looked agog. "Yew meen yew en't got no interest in creamin' up no dutty curny hoo-ers?"

Any response at all was nearly beyond possibility; however, I managed, "Perhaps in a short while, gentlemen."

"Come on now," Nate urged the driver. "Let's up'n find us that blondie!" & with that the 2 parted, but not before I was able to hear an adjunctive comment under his breath, "What'n tarnations's wrong with that there fella?"

"Durn't knew. Guess he's a qwee-uh-boy."

Nate strode off, chuckling. "Yee-ip! Bet that guy's had more blammed *dick* up his ass than I've had shit!"

Indeed.

Their own decadent laughter followed them as they edged into the crowd, ostensibly in search of the maladapted woman in the advertisement poster.

I turned to face a copiousness of activity. Amid "barkers," jugglers, dwarfs, stilted walkers, & petite gymnasts executing cartwheels before all, most of the crowd was fed at once into a wide lane that formed a clough betwixt everything, the carnival's main artery. Observation was my major intent (plus that candied apple) but so large was the crowd that I felt oppressed in spite of my desire to be here. With timidity, I took a single diffident step when—

"Sir, Sir?" a lithe voice made inquest from behind, & then a finger tapped my back.

I turned, startled. "Yes?"

Standing just behind me was a young blond woman-girl with deep Adriatic-blue eyes & a face whose sheer beauty shone like a beacon. Quite short, she stood, not much more than 5 feet; it only was after catching her arresting countenance that I noticed she stood on wooden crutches.

Her voice flowed like some aural honey. "First time at a carnival, Sir?"

"Why, um, no, though I suppose one might suspect that–I feel a bit out of place–"

"I think so," she chirped. "Mostly just red-necks here, and you're definitely not that!"

No, but red-necks DID bring me here, thought I with an inner smile. "I've been present at a few carnivals in the dim past, meager compared to this, however. And I did enjoy cotton candy once on Coney Island."

"Oh, we have that here–"

"And candied apples as well, I hope?"

"Of course!" she shrilled, eyes abeam at me.

At once I was enchanted, so enchanted in fact that my normally superior powers of deductive reasoning failed to make the most immediate coincidental observation. Her smile at me had slipped a trifle too high, revealing an absence of *teeth.* This could be no other than what the tall man's poster promised: Bliss, the Girl with Hands for Feet.

Recovering from the fruition, I immediately asked, "Might you direct me to its proper vendor, Miss? I'd be most obliged."

"About three-quarters down the midway"—she pointed into the crowd-stuffed passage—"on your left. I'd take you there myself, but I'm on poke-swiper watch."

"Pardon me?" I stretched the words.

She giggled, a becharming (and even–I'll own here– *erotic*) utterance. "That's why I called you, Sir. Your poke–you know–your wallet? Never carry it in your back pants pocket. Always in front instead."

A shock-reflex shot my hand back, where my billfold nearly hung halfway out of said pocket. "Poke-swipers" must be parlance for pick-pockets. How incognizant of me! I immediately enacted her counsel. "I cannot convey enough gratitude, Miss. The purity of your honestness could not be more axiomatic."

She giggled again. "My name's Bliss," she announced what I secretly already knew; with only a minimal difficulty, she extended a gracile, white hand whilst the pad of one crutch remained crooked into the joist of her arm & shoulder.

When I shook it I could've melted at its softness. My throat quivered. "I'm Howard."

She sighed as if in relief. "Howard–it's so good to meet someone smart and nice for a change! My *goodness!*"

"I'm flattered, Bliss," I replied, suspecting I'd blushed. "And what a delight it is to meet *you*," but then a strange despair fell over me, for I knew that once I departed for the candied-apple stand . . .

I would no longer be in her propinquity.

"I wish I could go with you, but . . . like I said"–and then she slumped on her wooden props.

"Of course, your employment here as a 'poke-swiper,'" I said, "demands your presence."

She nodded, losing half the smile.

I almost yelped when a massive hand landed softly on my shoulder. At once, I recognized the eloquent giant who spoke in fascinating antiquation: the poster-hanger.

"Fine esquire, be sartain of ye delight by my witness of thy coming into acquaintanceship with our loyal sarvant, Bliss."

"The delight is exclusively mine, Sir," I assured him.

"It is with a heart most complimented that I behold thee now, for trusting mine assurance of ye credulity of O'Slaughnassey's Travelling Show."

"My expectations are exceeded multitudinously, for your endeavor here is far more complete than any I've seen or imagined"–shrieks in the wake of a soaring roller-coaster shot my glance upward. "It's an astonishingly commendable show, indeed–and I'm most in debt to you for your generosity."

The titan man bowed hugely.

"And," I continued on a shocking impulse, "I am now *twice-fold* in debt, for my being here at your gracious invitation has bestowed upon me this opportunity"–I paused & looked directly into Bliss's deep-sea eyes–"to meet Bliss."

Now it was Bliss who blushed. The compliment seemed to have taken her aback, after which she seemed to blunder a response, "My friend here, Howard, was asking how to get to the candy apple stand."

Akin to magic, several 5-cent tickets appeared at the tips of the smiling giant's fingers; they were offered, then, to me. "Of this small token, excellent Sar, I beg thee to accept with all my gratefulness"–for the second time today, the generosity of this virtual goliath left me in an ebullient shock; however that shock would strike thrice when he supplied, "And it is Bliss who shalt accompany thee to ye sweet fruit which calls thy desire."

Bliss rose on her crutches. "Oh, thank you, Septimus!" she squealed.

Septimus! I thought. A great name from the earliest Colonial days! I'd have to use it.

The giant–Septimus–took Bliss's place as sentinel. Nothing could've made me more ecstatic, & in diction nearly as articulate as his, I rained more thanks, & Bliss & I were on our course–into the peopled turmoil of the "midway."

This woman-child struck me as one of the most graceful bearing, even on her regrettable crutches. *Crippled angel,* I thought in foggy muse. Suddenly my misgivings of the surly–indeed, the *red-neck*—throng dissolved as thin frost against morning sun. The soap-scent off Bliss's hair left me absolutely drunk with fascination & attraction; thus far, I hadn't even let my gaze stray past her shoulders, yet our crowd-wending now allowed me the ungentlemanly chance to pursue cursory examination. A fluffy white-cotton gown adhered with perfection against her the feminine curvatures; & it would be understatement to declare that her bosom thrust forward in abundance & an absolute lack of defect. This woman's presence left me in a thrall I could only describe as libidinally unrelenting; it is a fact, too, that I'd never been so densely *taken* by a woman, so psychically *arrested.*

The midway, as it's called, struck me as a dual-flowing river of chatty, malodorous humanity: a churning, bustling domdaniel leading to recesses unknown. We moved along with its course, myself nearly unaware of the closeness of so sullied a crowd. Prefatorial conversation commenced without delay: first my own provenance, then hers, though of myself I mentioned only that I was an antiquary & one having an interest in genealogy, the cosmological sciences, & a "devotee" of weird fiction. I did not reveal my entire name (not that any familiarity would likely strike her), nor that I had accrued a professional publishing history. Of herself, I learned that she'd been born but 19 years afore in the state of Maryland & a military town called Parole, "Where the Army prison used to be," she'd said. Her father had been in the Army, & had even been deployed to the mystery-shrouded province of Shannxi in exotic China.

"What," I asked, "prompted you into carnival life?"

She glided so effortlessly along on her crutches that scarcely a hitch was noticeable. "My husband *owns* the carnival. He has for years, and he's been really successful, even with the bad things in the economy."

"I may presume, then, that your surname is O'Slaughnassey?"

"That's right. I'd introduce you to my husband, but . . . " Whatever remained of her sentence dissipated like vapor, & her ever-present smile did as well.

The delay of cognizance shocked me. *Wait!* came my self-exclamation. *Her husband is the travelling show's possessor and presumably its topmost hierarch . . .*

I stared into the shifting crowd.

And Bliss is a prostitute . . .

At least that was the implication of the mechanic, Nate, based on testimony of a confidante. The deduction's implication gored me: O'Slaughnassey engages his *own wife* as a lady of the evening!

I quelled my outrage & continued to bear as if undistractedly enjoying our amble through the carnival's nerve-centre. Above us, like great, clanging, metallic beasts, the carnival rides spun, twisted, & soared while their driving motors beat a gusting staccato into the air. Passing on either side were stalls featuring a miscellany of either spectacles or gaming ventures—ring toss, shellgames, sledgehammers meant to be swung in an effort to raise a clanger to a bell & prove one's physical strength; soothsayers, "unnatural" medical specimens, contortionists, etc., etc.—which might otherwise have flagged my interest. Today, they did not, however. The entirety of my interest remained on Bliss.

Yet as she pursued more sundry talk, that beaconlike cast of her visage remained declined. I prepared to inquire of her sudden rupture of mood & aura, but—curse Pagana!–I lost my nerve as I so often had in the past. Meanwhile, as we made our way, various functionaries—"roustabouts" & "ride-jocks," factotums, stocky toughs who served as guards, roving custodians bearing brooms & mops like halberds–all of them grinned too *brightly* at her, & offered snippets of greetings that seemed to possess some connotation between the words. When one–a ticket-taker with an eye-patch & a shining bolus on his forehead–cracked, "Hey, Blissy? What say later, me'n you, huh?"

She replied with no more than a silent frown, & continued down the lane on her crutches.

"Oh, Howard . . . " She sighed in a way that slumped her gentle shoulders. "I don't know what to say."

"You needn't say anything unless it suits you. I'm very contented simply being in your company," & after I'd said that, I could hardly believe my bravado.

"You do know why Septimus let me leave, don't you? You must."

The question left me confused. "Why . . . I suppose to give you a break, and direct a customer to his destination, in this case, the candied apple vendor."

Several more strides on the crutches. Only then did I

glance at her feet, which did not extend as they should but instead appeared *rolled up.*

Like fists.

Stretched over them were white socks. *Hands down there,* I realised. *Not feet . . .* Eventually she went on, "But you've obviously met him before, so . . . you must know . . . "

A pause on my part. "Oh, yes, your friend Septimus appeared earlier at the repair garage, to post an advert."

She seemed startled, snapping a glance at me. "That's all?"

"Well . . . yes. It was the simplest matter, really. He affixed the poster, provided some tickets at no cost–a grateful excess of generosity, I must say—then was off in his motor."

"Did you . . . ," but she gulped as if disconcerted. "Did you see the drawing of me on the poster?"

"Why, no," I prevaricated with an immediacy that darkened my spirit.

"And Septimus told you *nothing* about me?"

"He mentioned you not at all."

"In here," she said hastily, & turned me through a narrow gap between a stall selling funnel cakes & that of a Negro woman whose forte was apparently the bending of spoons & other elongated metal objects, all by force of mind alone.

The compressed gap led us to a surprisingly silent nook created by several transport trailers squared off. Bliss struck flint to ignite several lamps whose odor told me they'd been filled with candlefish oil. Wan light exposed several tin cans of cigarette butts & crates serving as seats. "How convenient and comfortably secluded from the crowd," said I. "An area where workers–*carnies,* I'm sorry—may partake in respite."

Her face turned blank at my remark. More & more a cast of sullenness seemed to weigh her down on the wooden props. "It's what we call a 'possum belly,' Howard–"

"A *what?*"

"A possum belly. Don't know where that came from but that's what they're called."

I chuckled at the queer designation. "I'm sure I don't understand, Bliss."

Her expression remained blank. "A possum belly is a

secret place at a carnival, an area between trailers, an out-of-the-way tent, or even the storage compartments under the trailers themselves." She pointed to a bare mattress, befouled by stains, which was half-visible in the shifting dark. "It's a place where carny girls . . . can bring men to–you know. For money."

I tried to act unfazed. "Ah, I see."

"Do you really, Howard?" She sat on a crate, leaning the crutches aside. When I chose a farther crate, she reached up & snatched my wrist, a sub-verbal insistence that I sit, instead, next to her. Then she went on in the same agitation. "Girls come here to *hook,* Howard! And *I'm* one of them!"

The silence oscillated in the wavering oil light.

"That's why Septimus let me leave, to *work* you," & now a tear glimmered in her eye.

Work me, I let the words drool down some slope in my gut. "Bliss, I–"

Now that lovely, sun-bright face turned to stone. "I can't lie to you, Howard. I lie all the time, I *have* to! But I can't to you!" She began to cry openly. "I'm a *prostitute! I sell* myself!"

It was without conscious forethought that I took her hand. "Bliss. I don't care about such things–"

"Did you know?"

"Of course not," came my next lie, but what choice did this cringing circumstance leave me? "I don't care, and I don't engage in the assigning of judgments. I'm quite taken by you."

She collapsed in my arms, sobbing. "Oh, thank God, thank God! I knew He'd answer my prayer." Her svelte arms tightened about me. "You're so *different.* You remind me of the part of the world I can never have. To everyone else, I'm just a freak to *fuck.* I'm like–I'm like a spittoon–"

"Don't speak of yourself like that; it is an untenable circumstance which has effected your burdens." My own arm tightened about her as she continued to sob into my chest. The hair-scent dizzied me most pleasantly, & in spite of my determination *not* to regard her sexually, my chest constricted from an all-pervading rouse.

"I feel so good now–that you didn't know," her whisper slipped against my ear. "I thought–I thought you were just another john who'd . . . heard about me," & then she kissed me ever-so-daintily on my lips.

"Set your mind at ease, Bliss," I tried to console. "I could never in eons think of you in such terms; and, truly, I understand that in calamitous economic times, we must all engage in activities we otherwise wouldn't."

Her whisper continued to flow against my ear. "Many men come to me because, well, I have no teeth. It makes me . . . do certain things better. I was . . . born without them." I sensed that my being here for her to talk to gave her a much-needed comfort. "And then . . . my feet, too. I'd show you, but you'd be repulsed."

"Nothing relative to you, Bliss, could ever leave me repulsed."

She moved away in hesitation, stared off a moment, then lifted an attractive leg, displaying the white sock that seemed to sheath a fist. All I could say was, "Congenital anomalies, such as an absence of dentation, and developmental maladaptations of extremities are more common than you may think."

She looked at the fisted foot, began to reach forward. "They bill me at my show as having hands instead of feet but that's really not true." Then she removed the sock.

It was not a "fist" at the end of her svelte leg; in fact, it didn't appear to be a hand at all, but instead an aberrantly developed foot, smaller as if proper growth had been subverted, & rolled inward. "My father saw to it," she said dismally. "He'd been sent to fight the Boxers, in China, a long time ago, & he learned about 'foot-binding–'"

Immediately I winced at the outrage. I knew too well of this savage, subjugating procedure by which the feet of infant females were bound up to thwart proper growth; I'd seen sketches in several texts. It was a way to keep the female immobile & hence ultimately subservient. "In other words, your father inflicted you with this, after having seen evidence of its technique during his dispatch with the Army to rescue American diplomats and missionaries held by the Quing

Dynasty in the first years of the century."

In utter dejection, Bliss nodded.

My rage rose. A father who would deliberately bind her feet, & a husband who would sexually exploit her via her abnormalities? What kind of a world was this to allow such devilish things?

She put the sock back on, having apparently vented all she needed. At once, she was calm again, & continued to hold my hand. In phantasy, though, I pictured the most excruciating tortures for both her wretched father & beastly husband. "Oh, but we were going to the candy apple stand!" she remembered, & up she went, effortlessly on her crutches. Unable now to hold her hand, I kept it instead opened over the small of her back, an unconscious initiative for I felt *desperate* to sustain some modicum of physical contact. The effort seemed to please her as we plunged again into the beating human flux called the midway.

The apple vendor was soon discovered; subconsciously, I was about to order 2 but then winced when I remembered Bliss's absence of teeth. Next, we continued on our way, chatting innocuously; all the while, I forced myself to not contemplate the ordeal she would face later, via her "johns" & her "show." Toward the end of the midway's course there came a make-shift manner of cul-de-sac, featuring a trio of strongmen hoisting barbells of staggering size; & a "dunk-the-fool" game. But betwixt the last pair of stands, I glimpsed a personal trailer more exotic than any other & sitting higher. For a moment, a fancily carven door opened from which the trailer's occupant peered into the crowd. It was a gaunt, sallow-skinned older man in coattails, string tie, & blazing white vest. The thin, whiskery face looked incised, with heavily hooded eyes, & an overall mirthless countenance whose cast bespoke contented greed & measured callousness. I would guess the man to be in vicinity of 60.

"Oh, no," Bliss murmured. "Let's turn here, quick—"

I followed her lead, dismayed, noticing then that the coattailed man's subtly hateful gaze had fallen on us. "Bliss," I began, "that man in the exorbitant trailer seems to be–"

"Shhh! It's my husband. He'll thrash me if he thinks I'm lollygagging!"

"Thrash–"

"Howard, put your arm around me. If he thinks you're a john then he won't beat me."

I hardly had time to decipher her meaning, but did as asked. "This is crude," she said next, "but . . . you'll understand . . . ," & as we slowly made the turn, in full view of this wretched overseer O'Slaughnassey, Bliss stopped on her crutches a moment, kissed me quite lewdly, & also caressed my crotch for the briefest moment.

I tensed, my member reared like a teased beast. I could've fallen over at the sweet shock.

"Let's keep going now, quick!"

Dazed, I did as instructed. In the corner of my eye, I saw O'Slaughnassey disappear back into his trailer.

"I'm sorry, Howard," Bliss explained, strangely winded. "You don't understand the situation with my husband, but I had to do that because–"

"To project to your husband the pretense of going about the business that he forces you to engage in, yes–I understand." *To the Pit of the Shoggoths,* I wished O'Slaughnassy. To be sodomized by para-dimensional monstrosities forever would suit him just fine.

She sighed, but in relief this time. "I'm so happy you understand, Howard. I would never do such things if I wasn't stuck in this awful carnival."

"Of course, you wouldn't."

"If only I could hide enough of my earnings to get away, or . . . "

Get away, her words rolled in my head. A dream was already forming: that she *get away* . . . with me . . .

It was short work I made of the ambrosial candied apple, & lascivious thoughts indeed that occupied a recess in my mind, namely the image of myself giving oral ministrations to a panting & arch-backed Bliss while her strange compacted feet held the back of my head. Certainly, her climax would be all-encompassing, & just as certainly her delectable sex would taste sweeter than the apple. Ah, but what a ludicrous if not wholly uncharacteristic phantasy, eh? Following the throng's clockwise current, Bliss pointed out more of the show's prominent features; we hadn't yet traversed this side of the midway, & I found the pickings here more interesting &, I dare say, more outre. Better still, with Bliss as my escort, I was admitted to each specialty tent for free!

A small queue gathered about an elevated stage for one Hawberk, the Sword-Swallowing Man! First, objects less substantial disappeared down the artist's throat: a candle, glass shards, even a summer squash. Hawberk himself seemed older even than the wretch O'Slaughnassey but corded with cable-like muscles. Meager applause followed each demonstration, until one young heckler piped, "Aw, this ain't nothin'! I want my money back!" At this, Hawberk smiled & hefted finally a sword of extraordinary length, then dropped it into his mouth where it easily disappeared to the hand-guard. When he extracted it, the summer squash came with it–quite a trick–and the crowd applauded more heavily; but the brazen heckler's harassment did not abate. "Aw, I seen that trick a hunnert times at shows better'n this, old man!"

"Oh, have ye now?" Hawberk retorted. "So jest ye tell me, whippersnapper! Have ye seen better than *this?*" & in a sudden lurch, the oldster buckled over, & from his mouth shot a shimmering, 6-foot-long black snake which slapped hard on the floor, & the appearance of which sent half the crowd running for the exit & the other half jumping back several yards. The snake side-wound itself beneath the stage as applause rose like surf. It was quite a formidable spectacle, but outside Bliss chucklingly explained that 1) the brash heckler was actually a "shim," i.e., a low-order carnival employee whose insertion into the crowd was deliberate, & 2) the "snake" was really just a rubber prop whose exit was effected by invisible fishing line–visually believable thanks to the power of suggestion. In all, a wonderful illusion.

Other tents could less be described as "wonderful"; indeed, impressively grotesque was more along the mark. There was Betty, the Human Blood Vessel, or a relatively well-proportioned young woman wearing only tin cones over her nipples & the tiniest triangle of glittered fabric over her privates. What made her remarkable was this: a veritable *outbreak* of venousness, so complete that every square inch of exposed skin was webbed by beating blue veins; the deliberate coverage of her skin with oil intensified the effect to a gleaming hideousness. Next was a man who impossibly ejected both eyeballs from their sockets & switched them; & next, a woman billed to have been pregnant for seven years, her bare belly protruding no smaller than the volume of a medicine ball (Bliss later informed me that a benign tumor was responsible for her excessive abdominal girth, not pregnancy); & next, another performer I recalled from the advert: Cadaveressa, Revived From the Clutches of Death By African Magic! Espying this unfortunate woman in reality was far more disturbing than the sketched replication on the poster. She was literally a living skeleton, pallorescent skin stretched over bones, & a head like a skull dipped in pale waxen paint. The image was worsened by complete nudity, revealing emptied skin-flaps for breasts, & painfully jutting pelvic bones buttressing the fleshless groin & grim folium that could only be her sexual access-way. To Bliss I expressed my doubt that African Magic had anything to do with her condition but more than likely a willful abstinence from the consumption of food. "Oh, but, Howard," Bliss explained. "Her real name's Mary and she eats like a pig. It's just that she upchucks it all afterwards."

Charming.

Hence, the show's promised "oddities of nature." But then Bliss added as she crutched along, "You said you like weird things, Howard—"

"Weird tales of imagination, yes. It's curious to ponder exactly why such things are fascinating to some."

"Well, I just wanted to say, there's more"–she seemed to be smiling crookedly, as though hesitant–"but for that, you'd have to go to the Red Walk."

"The Red Walk?" I queried.

"The adults section. It's where I work."

We stood aside from the flow of boisterous passersby. Bliss

pointed to a larger tent egress guarded on either side by stolid-faced musclemen. RED WALK — 25-CENT ADMISSION. This must be the part of the show which housed the peep tents that Nate had referred to. & prostitutes & other lewd displays. *Where Bliss does her own show,* I sadly recalled.

"But please don't come to my tent, Howard," she appended. "I wouldn't feel right."

"I would never circumvent your wishes, Bliss," I assured her, remembering all-too-well Nate's brow-arching description. "And as for the other attractions . . . well, weird or not, I'm afraid they'd rupture my financial situation."

Her hand disappeared into a pocket, then she slipped me a lengthy strip of tickets.

"Why, Bliss, I could never–"

"Take them!" she whispered. "You're quite a gentleman but still a man. I want you to have a good time, Howard. Just . . . don't go to my tent." She batted her luxuriant lashes. "And I'm so hoping you'll stay awhile. I hope you can stay and see me again after my show's over."

"I shall do exactly that–"

Her expression intensified. "I'll only be an hour."

"Then an hour it is, Bliss. I'll meet you here at that time." The information seemed to elate her, while I was already more than elated by her desire to see me one last time. Before more parting words could be uttered, she kissed me quite passionately on the mouth, then ambled off on her crutches, disappearing beneath the canvas transom of the sinisterly named Red Walk.

Suddenly I stood alone behind the clamourous human tide, unnerved. Without Bliss's company I reverted to my misanthropic manner, on proverbial pins & needles. The woman-child's kiss left me painfully stoked, my privates gorged & damp from embarrassing leakage. A vertigo infected my vision; I was staring at the mysterious doorway which hinted at the most forbidden witness & promised grotesqueries far more potent than previous tents. Consciously, the idea of entering–even with the costless tickets–filled me with apprehension; yet now I found myself at the mercy of my *sub*conscious. I was utterly bereft of forethought when I approached the over-muscled lummoxes guarding the entrance, stoically handed over my admission, & stepped into eerie red-tinted darkness. It was not another tent I had entered, it was another world.

A world of shadow-shapes, wisps of sound, & unwholesome scents; a world of canvas corridors, wan red-lensed lamps, & prowling figures; of cringing desires, scintillant despair, & incognito transgressions–and it was into this undertow that I allowed myself to be sucked. Far more this place was than a den for deviates; it was a murk-ridden conclave of satyrs, incubi, & lust-daemons, which perhaps we all were beneath our brittle human faces. More strong-armed sentinels lined these cryptic passages, each fabric wall showing a line of lit dots from where peep-holes had been punched. "Piss party, right here, bub," one beefy sentinel notified; then another, "Dog show right in a-here, only two tickets." My belly seemed to prolapse at the insinuations. "What'sa matter, fella? Don't'cha wanna see a dog fuck a girl?" I staggered off, nearly stumbling. The most muffled squeals resounded with periodicity, then louder, ghostly moans. Indeterminate shapes that were men with their backs to me, staring into the eye-like holes, clearly masturbated as they feasted upon the visual delights within. When a hand firmly grabbed my shoulder, the tinted face of another sentinel warned, "Can't just loiter about, Mister. You can *look* or you can *do*, but both cost." He pointed to the channel's end like Dickens's spectre. "Doin's down yonder, a fin-bill and up, dependin' on what ya want. Lookin's here, for two tickets a peep." I could scarcely form words against my jaded daze. "In my lack of experience, perhaps you could make a recommendation," I stammered and conveyed the requested tickets. The block-shape of his face nodded. "I can tell by the way ya look, this 'un here'll float yer boat," he retailed and then urged me toward a glowing hole. Trembling, I peered in, only to be struck by an image like a cudgel's blow: a fat nude man on hands & knees, his back a veritable matt of fur; behind him knelt a younger, almost lissome man whose right arm lacked a hand. The larger one tensed as his rectum became a place of insertion for his collaborator's stump.

I tore my eye away & wobbled off. The miscreant sentinel chuckled.

For staying, for even *entering* this soul-dead place, I had only the deepest self-condemnation. But I knew why my darkest Id would not license departure. Bliss.

"Bliss," I demanded of one of the musclemen, wagging the string of tickets.

"She's doin' her show now," the spiritless voice grunted back. "Then she's off from 11 to 12. After that ya can turn a trick with her but ya gotta get on the list." He jabbed a finger down toward the area meant to serve as a bordello. "And the cost depends on what'cha want."

"Her show," I said. "Where?"

He snapped off 2 tickets & pointed to the next section of peep-holes, though most were already tenanted. In dreadful slowness, then, & in complete abandonment to my promise, I brought my eye to the hole . . .

Surely it was some imp of the perverse that forced my face to the ratty canvas. Through the hole I spied a circle of oil lamps guttering about a table on which a shinily naked Bliss lay reclined on her back. Her skin glowed like fresh white chocolate, her nipples plump & red as strawberries. The plenteous bosom rose & fell rapidly; she licked her lips & rolled her eyes in some cringing pleasure that at first alluded me, but then I noted the top of a man's head between her legs. The activity in which he engaged couldn't have been more lewdly apparent, along with the wet licking sounds which companioned the action. Yet while this ensued, all 4 of her limbs moved in an almost engine-like precision. This, Nate had already expounded upon: 4 more men stood at each corner of the table, lean, leering, naked men, displaying trenchant genital erections. They may as well have been faceless. The stout penises of the 2 men at her shoulders she stroked with her hands. The other 2 men she stroked with her deformed feet. The sound of this quatro of masturbation, coupled with that of the urgent cunnilingus, reminded me of ravenous animals feeding.

Perverse & unnatural as the spectacle may have been, my own arousal was almost too much to bear. The watchers to either side proceeded to manually satisfy themselves without inhibition. I was tempted myself but just couldn't bring myself to do so. Meanwhile . . .

Bliss's performance heightened my ability to inspect the severity of her foot-binding. I'd read of a variety of processes, yet hers was clearly the most grievous, her wicked father having clearly mastered the art. Her feet completely rolled in on themselves, which indicated that her arches & toes had been repeatedly broken & re-wrapped for the desired effect. A queer flexibility seemed evident as well–Bliss was able to adjust her "grip." All the while, the sheer weight of practice demonstrated her seamy, slatternly skill; her strokes picked up to a fever pitch, then at last all 4 men ejaculated on her at nearly the same time; indeed, the "climax" of the show.

Or was it?

When the spent men retreated out of view, there still remained the oral suitor whose ministrations continued. I could detect the rhythmic movement of the man's head, & the plot of blond fur just visible at his lip-line. Bliss kept her twisted feet aloft, her belly sucking in & out at manifest waves of pleasure; her hands cosseted her inflamed breasts, massaging the deposits of sperm all about in a glue-like glaze. She shrieked, then, & nearly curled into a throbbing human ball when her own climax broke. But when the quake of her release abated . . .

Her suitor rose.

It was Septimus, the colossan. His angly physique seemed to unfold as he, first, stood up, then climbed upon the table, hideously kneeling between Bliss's legs. Naked, this titan of a man looked otherworldly, a gut-sucked, long-boned creature more daemonical than human in aspect. The small, beady-eyed head declined from the long rack of bony shoulders, to intently spy Bliss's glazed nudity, & of his genitals.

They were as unnaturally huge as the rest of him.

The erection reared, a snouted serpent; as if on cue, Bliss fondled it with her misshapen feet, kneading drool from its terrifying tip, squeezing the meaty shaft with her unnatural clench. Then she awkwardly strained open her thighs & guided the foot-long-&-then-some organ into her sex–guided, I mean, with her foot. Septimus's gaunt form tensed as this aberration of the procreative act commenced. In slow, grueling strokes, the entirety of the penile shaft slid into the tiny, tender seat of Bliss's womanhood. One stroke after the next, all the way in, all the way out. At the finish of each insertion, Bliss reacted as if being reached into by an arm; her eyes bulged, her hips bucked, even her tongue indecorously jutted–all from the enormity of the violation. My own reaction from watching nearly dropped me into a swoon. Eventually, though, Septimus stepped up pace to the point of coital violence, begetting from Bliss's throat a staccato of shrieks amid the grotesque slapping of groins. Yet even in the obvious discomfort, the woman-girl plucked her nipples with one hand & dabbled desperately at her clitoris with the other, somehow milking pleasure from what must have been eyeball-rolling pain. However, more than pleasure was milked next, when, sensing imminent crisis, Septimus withdrew the monstrous organ, hitched forward, & then Bliss's deformed yet adroit feet masturbated the pulsing shaft as she herself leaned closer with eyes closed & mouth opened. A literal salvo of opalesescent spurts emptied directly into her mouth–an inhuman volume. Then the single throb of her throat signaled her swallowing it all.

When I backed away from that awful peep-hole–truly the eye of Hell–I dazedly noticed all of the other peepers had departed, leaving lines of their own spent seed on the tent canvas. The madness of what I saw–indeed, the madness of this *entire wretched enterprise*–left me mad myself, mad as a babbling alley vagrant. Common sense was now beyond my ken; at once, I knew what I must do: I must somehow smuggle Bliss out of this infernal place, & take her away forever. I would spirit her away to Providence with me. I would discover some way to see to it that her life of forced debauchery at the hands of her petty satrap of a husband would be over forever. I would find a way to support her even in the harsh light of the

47

truth that I could barely support myself.

Oblivious now to the roiling crowd & boisterous chatter, I waited outside the entrance of the execrable Red Walk, my mind's eye bruised from the outrage of what I'd witnessed inside. An hour's time had passed since our last meeting, & an hour was what she'd asked me to wait. An utter nervousness overcame me. What would I say? How could I convince Bliss–a beautiful woman in spite of her disabilities–to come away with me, a writer of the poorest strata, a spindly form & otherwise unemployable recluse & none-too-handsome nervous wreck?

But the hour had passed, then so did half of the next one, yet Bliss had not yet shown herself. I began to pace back & forth along the midway's edge, oblivious to the barkers, jugglers, stilt-walkers, etc., deaf to the screaming clang of railed thrill-rides thundering overhead. Soon it was as though my volition had been expropriated by some supernatural agency, & when my watch told me Bliss was now more than an hour late, said agency puppeteered me back into the guarded maw of the Red Walk. Blank-faced, I paid another entrance fee, then waded through the familiar red-lit murk. "Back again, eh, Mister?" one of the rousters jawed at me. "So it seems," I replied, then he: "Back for more lookin', or is it *doin'* you're after now?" "Doing," I blurted. "Previous counsel has led me to believe that time with a woman can be arranged at the end of the walk. Might this be true?" "Previous counsel, huh?" the ruffian chuckled. "If you got the copper in yer pocket, yeah. Down there. They got gals who'll do things ta yer willy you ain't never thought of." I passed him then, as though his very existence had expired, cantering my way to the terminus of the carnal labyrinth. The tent-flap leading to what could only be the bordello seemed to glide toward me rather than me toward it, where the largest of the musclemen stood guard, massive arms crossed. One side of the brute's face was scar-lined; in a pure Irish dialect he asked, "Top a the evenin' to ya, Sir. What'll it be?"

"Bliss," I said.

"Aye, she'd be for all of us if we had our way, but not for

you, not tonight."

In an instant, I grew enraged. "And why *not,* Sir? This is a business enterprise, is it not? Where the company of a woman may be procured in exchange for funds deemed sufficient?"

"Oh, I know what it 'tis you're after, lad. A dick-suckin' from Bliss is a sweet deal indeed, and she's sucked mine on many occasion–and likewise sucked on my billfold as well"– he laughed, while I remained deadpan. "Aye, you must'a heard that she's got not a tooth in her mouth."

"She was born without them, yes——he informed me of that."

An accented laugh rumbled like tumbling stones. "That may be what she told ya, man, but the truth is O'Slaughnassey himself pulled all them choppers out years ago."

The words turned me to stone. "He . . . deliberately . . . pulled them . . . out?"

"A'course, lad! Once he married her proper, that is. She weren't but a lass of twelve or so back then–well, maybe eleven. But with her feet the way they is, she gets every pervert this side of the pond sweet on her, and that dandy mouth with no teeth in it?" He laughed aloud. "Don't tell me you ain't been thinkin' about it. O'Slaughnassey's a right smart man. Yankin' them out made her the best dick-sucker this show's ever seen. He makes more money whorin' her than he makes the rest'a the whores all together, that he does."

The bruiser's grinning face seemed to contort into something half-Mephistopholian. I hoped, even prayed, that his horrendous exposition was just a carnal-house lie, but somehow the sheer evil in his cast told me it was not.

It was truth.

& with that truth, I could've collapsed, muttering aloud my own despair. "What kind of a world could let such horrors be? The girl is pure innocence, yet fate gave her a father that bound her feet & a husband who pulled her teeth? Surely the cosmos should prolapse and suck this pest-warren of a planet into abysmal voids of uncreation–"

But now the Irish brutarian laughed all the more. "Oh, Mister–you yanks are somethin', aye? We ain't all from New

England, ya know. How is it ya can be so hot on Bliss while ya know nothin' about her?"

"I assure you, *Sir*," I snapped, "that I am *not* in reception of your meaning."

"Things are different all over. See, Bliss's father and her husband are one in the same," & then the bout of laughter redoubled.

Evil, evil, evil, I thought, wanting to vomit. To hang myself summarily would've been better than learning this. My voice trembled along with my hands when I demanded, "That may well be, Sir—nevertheless I insist on purchasing an allotment of time by which I may share in some of her company." I emptied my billfold & shook my entire stack of notes at him. "How *much?*"

"*No* amount of money is enough tonight—"

My ire grew to full-scale rabidness. It was not even a "trick" I wanted, but only a few moments to convince her to come away with me, not that I could have told *him* that. "What's *that* supposed to mean! Is there something *irregular* about me? How is it that shylocks such as you & your 'carny' brethren refuse hard cash?"

"Best to let your dander down, lad," the rapscallion adjured gregariously in spite of the nihilistic cast. "Your money's good as the next one's, but Bliss won't be turnin' no tricks tonight on account of—" but before the explanation's remainder could be made sonant, a brief commotion ensued from the darkness of the adjoining canvas corridor, then from the murk emerged 2 more overly muscled toughs.

They were bearing a makeshift stretcher fashioned from heavy sheets of fabric wrapped about 2 poles; upon this lay a wan form beneath some sheets.

No, no, no, my psyche groaned even before my eyes registered the truth. It was *Bliss* who lay crumpled, shivering, & battered upon the stretcher.

"What in the name of all things decent happened!" I yelled.

A large hand opened over my heart & pressured me back. "You keep yer dander down, man, else I'll be introducin' your kisser to my fist. Bliss got a bit of a pranging is all—"

Spittle flew when I yelled further, "A *pranging?* Someone's beaten her senseless!" & as I made the exclamation, she was carried briskly past me, one eye swollen closed, her cheek a grotesque purple contusion, mouth crimson with blood. In that last irreducible fraction of a second that I saw her, her good eye opened, bloomed at the sight of me; then she smiled & susurrated "Howard . . . "

Then she was taken away, & I knew, somehow, that I would never see her again.

"Why was she beaten?" I pled. "What could someone so filled with benevolence as Bliss have done to incur such wrath? Was it a customer–er, I mean, a john, a trick, or whatever it is you call it?"

"Wasn't no john, my good fellow. See, Bliss's job when she's not doin' her peep-tent is to work johns'n turn tricks. Earlier today, when she *should'*a been haulin' in some possum-belly quickies before her show, the lazy tart was loiterin' about & squandering time with some fella she had eyes for—"

"Some . . . fella?" I questioned, my throat going dry.

"Aye, 's'what I heard. Whores do that on occasion, turn a lotta tricks, make a lotta cash, then they start gettin' a big head'n thinkin' they're somethin' special. Specially the good ones, the ones like Bliss that can suck a dick like dicks never been sucked or lay a fuckin' on a man so good he just can't get her out'a his head so's he keep comin' back over'n over'n over again, handin' over his cash. That's Bliss, see? Every so often, she gets ta takin' her life for granted, forgettin' that she wouldn't *have* no life if'n it weren't for Mr. O'Slaughnassey marryin' her."

Of all the interminable outrage; all the diabolic *abuse.* My blood seemed to crackle in my veins as my guts sunk deeper & deeper as if into a bottomless pit of roiling bitumen.

"So," the Irishman continued, "you can understand that she was properly punished. No bones was busted, and nothin' of her insides was broke accordin' to the doc. She just got mussed up a bit is all."

Mussed up. The words curdled my stomach. This human animal perceived women as mere property, as pets to be utilised for profit, & when they misbehaved, they were *mussed up.* Had I a revolver, I surely would've emptied it into this bounder's noxious face. But the worst insinuation was already festering in me as a malignant growth. "And you say that she was beaten for squandering time with . . . some 'fella' in particular?"

"Some skinny chap was all I heard. She didn't even *try* to work him for a trick. Had *eyes* for him, even though she's married proper."

The "skinny chap," of course, *had* to be me. Hence, *I* was the primary cause of her unspeakable beating.

I wished for that revolver again, to put, this time, to my own head.

"So's get'cher mind off Bliss, lad, and take your pick of one'a our other lovely whores. We got *all* kinds'a doxies, just you believe it–ah, there's one now!" & down the insubstantial corridor I momentarily glimpsed a willowy strumpet with bare breasts like white cupcakes on her chest. She disappeared into a flap. "That lass there, Sir, is called Squeegee, and she's as fine a place ta drop your baby-batter as you'll find."

"*Squeegee?*" I asked, perplexed as to the name.

"Pussy *so tight,* when your John Thursday's sluggin' in and out of it"–he nodded–"makes a sound like cleanin' winda's, it surely does."

"How . . . unrepresentative," I offered.

"All our harlots, my friend, are fine as bloomin' China. Not a schlupper among 'em."

My curiosity left me unable to resist. "Schlupper?"

"Aw, lad, are ya daft! A gal that while's you're fuckin' her? Her pussy makes a sound like soldiers marchin' through mud. Schulp-schulp-schulp. You know?"

"How . . . majestic . . . "

"My point is, when one'a *our* lasses is done with ya? You'll not have a drop'a sap left in the two balls God put in yer sack."

This man is deplorable, I thought with the sharpest of frowns. But before I had time to decline, footsteps were heard, & from the adjoining corridor, an ectomorphic, stooped figure proceeded. At once, my vision was riveted.

The coattails, string tie, & white vest seemed to shout at me, as did the thin face & hooded eyes.

"Why, Mr. O'Slaughnassey," the Irishman greeted. "Now that you've got the wife back in line, perhaps you'd care for a nip." He produced a vulgar hip flask.

The 60ish show owner's voice creaked like old timbers. "No, McMullen, I'm tipsy enough from the joy of beatin' that cunt'a mine silly, don't cha know?"

"I'm sure I do, Sir. And it 'twas as fine a beatin' as I've seen in a long while."

"The more ya do for 'em, the more they lie and connive. Leaves a man no choice but ta bloody 'em up."

"Aye, Mr. O'Slaughnassey."

The hooded eyes turned to me. "And what a coincidence *this* is! I'll be damned if the gentleman to your side is not the same scoundrel who wasted so much of Bliss's time earlier, and cost me money!" His bony finger pointed right at me.

Odd as it seems, it was not trepidation that ensnared me, but a very pure & unadulterated furor. The sight of this treacherous man–a father who would marry his own daughter, cripple her, & pander her out; indeed, the very man who'd just beaten Bliss unmercifully–sent my wits asunder, leaving only my physical body fueled by the rage of humankind's ancestral days of half-ape barbarity. I flew past the Irish ruffian, & in a second had my hands about O'Slaughnassey's thin neck, spitting words of venom, "An abomination you are! A slime of the worst of human effluence from the bung-port of Hell!" I began to squeeze the thin neck. "May a *pox* be on you, you who would maim & molest your own daughter solely for profit in this flesh market that can only be described as *luciferic!*" but just as my grip would tighten in this crazed phantasy of strangling the wretch, fists the size of grapefruits battered me from behind until the entire world was spinning about me.

"A right rat bastard this one is, Sir," I heard the Irish accent through head-pounding fog. My face was in the dirt.

"There's one in every crowd, my good Irish."

"Aye, and did ya know that he was workin' me for info about your wife?"

"Hmm. Knowing that, I'll have to beat her all the harder."

"The whole job for 'im, Sir?"

"For scum like this, we should let the dogs have at his cock and balls, but, no, McMullen. This droog counts for naught–for less than what's on the corncob after I wipe—and as easy as the police are to pay off, I've not the patience for the inconvenience. He's a mere fly-speck, not worth a good man's time or effort to set straight. Just throw him off the property."

"With pleasure, Sir!"

"But first . . . "

The collision of the Irish fists to my head had me seeing double. But the next collision was not from a fist at all, but O'Slaughnassey's heavily booted foot.

Directly to my groin.

"Here's a good one to remember me by . . . " A wizened laugh. "I'll say, McMullen, all this violence has my old dog up and barking. I think I'll go to Bliss's trailer now and knock her about some more, then put some vintage cream up her backside." His foot roughly nudged my wobbling head. "You hear that, Yankee scum? For raising a hand to me, I'll keep Bliss uglied up for a good long time. Think about that."

I believe his words caused me actually to vomit. Pain cocooned my body, & amid a dark, accented chuckle, I was carried off much the same as a sack of refuse. My consciousness winked in & out, & the agony betwixt my legs existed as an entity of its own. I thought sure that my testes had been ruptured to slush.

I saw only in mazed blinks: inquisitive faces, staring eyes, agape mouths. I was hauled out of the carnival's entrance & dropped to the ground, heart hammering. Senseless, I heard an abrasive sound—

Kuuuuur-HOCK

—as the surly thug spat copiously into my face.

"A fresh Irish oyster for ya, lad, with my compliments. And if you're stupid enough to ever come back here? Ya won't be leavin' alive."

The rogue tromped off, his laughter like the peals of a satanic bell.

Many minutes passed before I could reconstruct my wits. Bloody-faced & half-blind, I stumbled away from the staring crowd that waited for admission. Ahead of me: the vast field of scrub crammed with motor-cars & the smear of twilight-tinged sky. One hand to my head, the other to my groin, I staggered away; away from that screaming, hadean dervish-saturnalia; away from the leering, sin-faced throng; forever away from O'Slaughnassey's Travelling Show . . . I knew not what crested most precipitously in my spirit: my humiliation, my rage, or my horror for Bliss. Would that malefactor O'Slaughnassey really beat her further for sport? Would he anally rape her as he'd implied, & keep her "uglied up" because I'd assaulted him? The prospect made me moan in the most fathomless despair.

Relocating Nate & the unbecoming bus driver was akin to the needle in the haystack proverb; so, too, was the prospect of finding Nate's claptrap vehicle. Instead–always one given to lengthy walks–I stumbled straight away from the carnival's noise, crowds, & infernal lights, re-taking the unpaved road that had delivered me to this pit of lust, thievery, & con men. Soon the wicked din was far behind; & each of my strides away grew longer & more stable. I wiped my bloodied face with my handkerchief, regaining my breath, as reason soon returned to my mind. Ache as my testicles did, a painful but brief physical inspection assured me they'd not been ruptured. *The police!* I resolved. What other course did I have? Once I returned to the garage, I could use the telephone to call. But then the prospect dwindled. In uncharted backwoods such as these? A domain of "rubes," "red-necks," & "crackers?" Local police were surely prone to corruption; O'Slaughnassey himself said that he had them in his pocket. *It's my word against theirs, and I'm the outsider here,* I knew. The police would likely arrest me on a trumped up charge, taking payment to do so. Now I felt hopeless.

Was there no other course I could take?

In my soul I was at war with myself. Where there was no justice, a real man could effect his own. The greater segment of my conscience wanted nothing more than to return to that dreadful, evil-imbued carnival—that cauldron of greed & indulgence & lechers—infiltrate its perimeter, & then . . .

Find O'Slaughnassey and kill him.

A real man, yes, but was I such a man? A soft-handed scribe lacking brawn & bravado? Could I really depart from my sheltered & sensitive ways & be the crusader who ended Bliss's life-long terror?

I stared at the moon as if awaiting an answer, yet none was forthcoming.

Plodding steps took me back the way I'd come, along the dense woodline, while a strange dirge-like litany played in my head–a litany to failure. I knew I'd be back at the garage in little more than an hour's time, but what then? To pass a sleepless night on the immobile bus, to fret over Bliss & what her perverse father/husband was doing to her? A dense, nearly deafening chorus of crickets & night-birds accompanied the dirge in my head, yet over time, these natural sounds of wildlife ceased. I stopped, taking notice of the silence that shouldn't be. & then?

Commotion.

From the woods, frenzied shouts rose at a distance, but closer came a deliberate thrashing, as of madly running feet through brambles. It all transpired so fast I could scarcely react. & next:

"Good God!" I shouted.

From the woods a blocky frantic figure shot out: a man obviously being chased, for in the background those other voices increased in tenor; I heard rough accented exclamations, the likes of "Don't let the varmint git away!" "Which way'd he go?" "Toward the fields, I reckon!" & "Pray the Lord on High we don't lose him!" Yet the man to which these voices referred, the frantic figure, had just bolted from the woods & was heading right toward me. The moonlight revealed the terrified face of an unkempt, wild-haired man of about 40, his eyes inflamed by a wedding of madness & panic-fear. I don't think he saw me on the road for he kept running straight, shooting glances behind. Then a voice boomed in the background, clearly addressing me: "You there on the road!

In the name'a God stop that fella just run out the woods! He done raped'n murdered a *child!*" The words had not even consciously registered in my brain before my arms shot out & in what must have been complete surprise "clotheslined" the alleged murderer. It was the inside of my elbow that caught him directly across the throat. There was a gargled grunt, then the figure flew backward against the unseen obstruction, & landed hard on his back.

Half a dozen brawn-stocked men of the sort that are known as "hillfolk" surrounded the scene with guttering torches. The fallen man foundered at their feet, groaning.

A hand callused like sandpaper slapped my back to the extent that I nearly lost my breath, then a hardy voice in the local dialect boomed, "Sir, we are, I say, we are in some tall debt to ya for so bravely stoppin' this white-trash killer in his tracks! The bastard almost got away!" & at once the entire rustic group chattered their thanks & shook my hand. It was the first hillman who shook my hand, though, with the vigour of a well-pump. "My name's Eamon Martin, and these all's my kin, other Martins, Tucktons, Bishops mostly. We live out yonder in the woods, preferrin' not to mingle much with the outside world, seein' how evil it's a-gettin'." The alleged fugitive was hoisted up by 2 well-muscled men in overalls, then shaken around. Perhaps the power of suggestion impelled me, but the face on that man in the torchlight was truly a face filled with malevolency. He wore heavy-fabric'd garb with a # stitched on the shirt; that along with the iron ring about his ankle left no doubt as to his status: an escaped convict. "This pile'a swamp-rat shit must'a been in a chain-gang'n managed ta bust his shackle. Then he come through where we all live and-and . . . ," & then Eamon gulped in a choked sadness. "Ain't no doubt'a his devilish crime 'cos it was Constance Butler, the preacher's wife, who done caught him in the act. Rapin' the high heaven out'a li'l Sary May Boover, and when he done got his nut, he up'n raped Constance too. But poor Sary weren't but thirteen, and he busted up her insides so bad, the poor girl bled to death."

"That's-that's horrible," I croaked. "And it seems that

such eye-witness testimony verifies this man's guilt beyond all doubt."

"That it does, Sir. And now's time for us ta right as much as we can, while's all we can do is pray for young Sary's immortal soul. Foller me, it'd be our pleasure to at least offer ya some refreshment."

Amid my own calamities, I was about to decline the rustic's offer of hospitality, but suddenly I was aware of a mighty thirst, and I think I could trust in my judgment of men that these hillfolk were sincere. So I accepted, and followed.

Eamon & the entire group then wended their way back into the over-nourished forest, torches bobbing. "Mind yer fire men, and take care," Eamon ordered, then to me, "Ain't but a short walk, Sir. Now I can tell by lookin' at ya that you're a man of some soffister-kay-shun, likely a *city* man, am I right?"

"I'm from Providence, Rhode Island, yes, and I appreciate the compliment."

"No, Sir, 'tis *us* who 'preciates *you* takin' down this akker-lite'a the devil. He'd shorely be gone now weren't it fer yer bravery."

"Really, it was mostly luck, I must admit; I did little more than throw my arms out to catch him in the throat."

"Aw, yer too humble, Sir! Ya stopped a godless monster in his tracks! But bein' a city fella, there's things ya need ta understant. Down here, see, the way the world is leaves us no choice but to take care'a our own. The police? Shee-it, they ain't no better'n common criminals theirselfs. And what I'm a-gettin' at is city ways don't work out here, only backwoods ways is what works. What's right is right–it's that simple. You follerin' me, Sir?"

"I believe you're referring to the tenets of what's colloquially known as 'Jungle Justice,' or the proper engagement of the law where there *are* no formal laws," I said.

"Only laws anyone needs is these laws here," & from a pocket the big man produced a weathered Bible. "'A eye for a eye,' it says. Don't need no fancified big-city lawyer ta tell what *that* means."

In spite of the situation's gravity, I smiled at the man's

simple yet unblemished morality. "No, one most assuredly does not."

A big finger accentuated his words. "All's I'se tellin' ya this fer is so ya know, in case what'cher 'bout ta see comes ta be too much fer ya."

I followed, thinking deeply. Did he mean I was about to witness an execution? Part of my upbringing's urbanity told me how wrong this was, but who was I to judge? Who was I to condemn? This was another world, far apart from me, & possibly more genuine than mine. I had no right to interfere or to post objection. & besides . . .

I *wanted* to see this creature die. In all honesty? I would *thrill* to watch a child-killer swing at the end of a rope.

Deeper & deeper we wended into the dim, tunnel-like forest. How Eamon could remember each twist & turn amazed me; it was a nighted maze with no visual points of reference, yet in a short while our steps disgorged us into a spacious clearing of pin-drop silence lit by torches mounted on sticks, & amid all this congregated at least a dozen more hillfolk, men & women, all dowdily dressed, still, & blank-faced. When they saw that the culprit had been captured, a collective sigh seemed to issue like a gust of timid breeze.

"We got him!" Eamon announced, then turned to me. "And it was this fella here who done it."

All eyes homed on my face.

Were these the "creekers" that Nate had spoken so lewdly off? Many of the bumpkinly women were quite comely & robust-bosomed, & appareled in scant sewings of cloth that revealed much of their shapely physiques. Did some of them eye me with wantonness after Eamon, clearly the clan's foreman, had announced my participation in the scoundrel's capture? No, the notion was absurd. What *must* have I been thinking?

A canteen derived from an animal duodenum was thrust before me–crude but effective. I upended it & poured cool spring water into my mouth. There was no gainly way to do this but the drink was much needed & heartened me at once.

"Step on over, boys," Eamon cracked again, & as if from

thin air 2 smudge-cheeked boys appeared, sheepishly looking down. "This here is . . . Why, I didn't catch'yer name, Sir."

"Howard," I said.

"This here's *Howard,*" he addressed the boys, "and a very brave man he is."

"Really, it was nothing," I reiterated uncomfortably. "More luck than–"

"Howard, I am a mite *honoured* ta introduce ya to my two boys, Clonner'n Jake. Clonner's six, Jake's five."

"Fine young men, both of you," I addressed the lean children & shook their small hands. "And it is a stalwart and just-minded man indeed that you two have for a father."

Oddly, the boys seemed impressed by my presence, perhaps even awed; then one of them stepped forward to stammer, "Yuh-you up'n catched the devil-man who done that horriblest thang ta Sary?"

"That he did, Jake, and all'a our folk can now sleep easy on account'a it," Eamon said. "Howard's from the outside world, the *city,* so's you two can see not *all* city folks is all balled up like most."

"The city has its attributes, true," I said, "but it seems to me that truly *genuine* living is far better experienced in the cusp of nature, as you two excellent boys have the privilege of knowing firsthand."

Eamon wagged a finger. "Now you boys listen ta Howard, 'cos what he says is right," & then he smiled proudly. I was about to make more discourse with the 2 lads, but the sudden sound of footsteps crunching thicket resounded about the clearing. All our glances snapped over, then, when in a Stygian gap betwixt 2 shaggy trees, a pair of men appeared, solemn-faced as the others, each bearing an end of a wooden table, clearly hand-hewn.

"It's time, Eamon," intoned an older man amongst the congregation; perhaps this would be the clan's elder.

Eamon nodded. "Clonner, Jake, run along back the shack now."

"Aw, but Paw," whined the younger one. "Cain't we stay'n have a gander?"

"Yeah, Paw," implored the other, Clonner. "We wanna watch the—"

It was the power of Eamon's stare that cut the plea off effective as a knife through a sausage. "This here's grown-up tendin's, and ya both know it. Don't make me tell ya agin, lest we'll'se be visitin' the woodshed."

"Yes, Sir," the boys whispered in concert. I bade them both farewell, after which they obediently scurried away.

"Fine, fine boys, indeed," I said. "In their eyes I see initiative, fortitude, and accountability."

"That's dang kind'a you to say, and I'se shore they'se made finer still by a-meetin' you. I pray God some'a it rubs off."

Eamon's compliments had kept me sidetracked; so had the admiring glances from the other female "creekers." It was uncanny. I knew that I was the curiosa here, the metropolitan in the midst of backwoodsers, yet hardly a hero. I noticed one young woman in particular, a fascinating albino with pinkish eyes & clearly the most curvaceous build of all the other women. Her high, plump breasts seemed hammocked on her chest by the merest patch-works of fabric, while her groin was covered by stitched clippings of denim barely ample enough to hide all the intricacies of her privates. From there, long, immaculately toned legs descended to petite, unshod feet; & the waist-edge of her shorts hung so low that several strands of whitish nether-hair escaped their boundaries. Perspiration misted the exposed midriff. Her eyes held fast on mine, then she daintily licked her lips . . .

My, I thought.

But it was the pair of table-haulers that reclaimed my attention. Something heavy was insinuating itself upon the clearing, something heavy in an abstract sense, intangible as it was grave. Eamon directed the haulers to "Set 'er down right smack-dab in the middle, men," & then the table was placed in the center of this eerie torch-lit nook. "The table," I uttered. "Is the killer to be—" but before I could finish with the word "decapitated," Eamon said, "It's how things're done in this sitch-er-ay-shun, Howard, and how they'se *been* done fer a long, long spell. There ain't no justice less'n the *worst'*a crimes are righted by the *worst'*a punishments." He looked at me stolidly. "'A eye fer a eye'."

I nodded, holding my inquisitiveness. Decapitation certainly seemed in order for such a monster, yet I sensed this was not to be; & when I looked again, I noted that said monster had been gagged & then securely lashed to the table with stout sisal.

"It's how things're *done,*" Eamon added in a softer tone. "It ain't city ways, but it's *right* ways," & with that cryptic remark, he deputed himself to the table as all the watchers seemed to huddle together to watch now: the men keen-eyed & sobersided, while the women seemed quietly enlivened. Some seemed nervous in a paradoxical anticipation, holding hands, even trembling.

Did the torchlight faintly dim? Slowly a shroud of the primeval settled over the gathering & above all else, a silence that was spectral, a mood like watching some anciently tribal funerary. Yet this was no burial, this was an execution.

"Good folks'a the land, good folks'a God," Eamon began to all, his voice carrying. "May we all pray fer the precious soul'a our Sary May Boover who was taken from us so horribly." Everyone bowed their heads then; eyes closed & lips offering unvoiced supplication. After a flickering pause, Eamon went on. "'Tis true that this was a awful happenin' to occur but 'tis truer that the Lord our God works in mysterious ways so's that no bad death kin ever really be *bad,* because in death come life eternal." Eamon's burning eyes looked then to me. "And may God bless 'specially the newcomer, Howard, whose bravery saw fit ta end the horror that the Prince'a Darkness done dropped inta our midst . . . "

The silence thickened uncomfortably as so many sets of eyes looked at me in assuagement, gratitude, & even wonder.

"And may God bless us all'n give us the dang *strength* ta live in His ways, be good ta those good ta us, and ta do what's *right* in the dag-blasted face'a evil!" Eamon's sudden exclamation reverberated through the woods.

All but I tensed when Eamon ended his oratory & surefootedly approached the table on which the captive shuddered. For a moment, un-infringed silence fell, such that the convict's very heart could be heard beating frantically in his rising & falling chest, a muffled yet somehow *whining* staccato. The monstrous man's corrupted eyes blazed as he gnawed the gag. Eamon's head bowed in a final unspoken prayer, then in a gesture that seemed ritualistic, one of the congregation parted without noticeable instruction.

It was the shapely albino, & I must admit my own heart surged faster at my seeing her. Nature had uniquely paled the pinkish skin with a tone like deep fog; that & the odd sprawl of crinkly grey-tinged reddish hair on a woman so rife with youth gave her a sexually alien aura, in unison with the rest of her physical nomenclature which could only be regarded as supreme. It was not my nature to apprise women with such intent physical awe (I'd done the same with Bliss, though not so overtly) but now, in this foreign scenario, this unbeknownst recess of peopled wilderness . . .

I could not help myself.

The woman's sheer *mammiferousness* must be singing the same song to every man in the clearing, her perfect legs sleek; her taut but spacious buttocks flexing with each noiseless step forward; & the breasts rocking in the spare hammock of fabric were enough to break a monk's vows. I had to tear my eyes off the young woman to keep from seeming a lecher; only then did I notice that in this unsignaled dispatch to the table, she'd brought an implement with her.

A mallet.

I believe it was a hubbing mallet: a jar-sized striking-head (more than likely hickory), padded with thick leather. *What on Yuggoth could* that *be for?* the tool's appearance forced me to wonder. In a motion somehow reverent, the albiness passed the mallet to Eamon, then lithely turned to depart; before returning to her place in the circle, though, she painted me with a glance that seemed famished, but I mean famished in a *wanton* way.

The eerie atmosphere left me wont to believe that everyone in attendance knew what was about to take place–everyone but me. The sense of expectancy became semi-palpable, like heavy wood-smoke, & there seemed a briary static in the air which raised gooseflesh. It was my inclination that Eamon had spoken his final words before this primal rite of execution commenced. Would he stove in the culprit's skull? Fracture his bones? What other use could there be for a mallet in so aboriginal a scenario?

I blinked. Keyed as I was with curiosity , impulse shot my eyes toward the albiness. No longer was she appraising me; she was intent on the table—

Whack . . .

I jerked at the less-than-substantial sound, which seemed a restrained impact followed by a sonic flatness–it's the only way I can describe it. I refocused on the epicenter . . .

The convict shuddered as if convulsant upon the stout table. What had happened?

Whack . . .

The sonic *flatness* again, but now I'd gleaned its source. Eamon had vised the killer's head down against the table by pressing his large hand against the fear-shocked rictus, & with his other hand very meticulously buffeted the crown of the culprit's skull with the mallet. Yet even this second blow did not cause death, & this mystified me. Was not death the goal of an execution? Eamon's mallet-strikes were clearly charged with *finesse,* not determinate force.

Now the convict's violent, heel-thumping convulsions weakened to a low shivering. Meanwhile, Eamon had disposed of the rough tool & produced a smallish knife in order to . . .

What IS this? I thought.

The big backwoodsman crouched over &, with a sharpened focus & steady hand, dragged the knife-tip around the top of the head in the attitude of a headband. Instantly, a thread-like crimson line appeared, & following this inexplicable action . . .

My eyes bulged.

Eamon righted his stance, worked his stubby fingers under the incision he'd just effected, & without forethought peeled the culprit's scalp off the skull.

My conscious mind escaped me now, leaving only a

leftover of sentience, which the silence amplified. The psychic drone that pestered me previously now howled banshee-like in my head.

My head, I say, while however the execution's most salient feature was clearly the head of the now-deceased child-murderer/escaped convict. The top of the bare skull at this point of progression showed blaringly as the ravaged scalp was flung away. The impact of the mallet was now plain: the boned dome remained intact yet slightly imploded, & webbed by cracks. Eamon engaged the knife-tip to aggravate the webbing & disturb what remained of the dome's now unsound integrity, after which he began to pluck out the pieces of fractured bone.

Why, I wondered. *Why?*

This indisputably reasonable enquiry–little did I know then–would be answered posthaste.

Eamon's barbarous onus left an opened jigsaw of the skull-top, producing a roundish opening where the bone-pieces had been. Within, the convoluted meat of the white-pink brain was easily viewed, showing beneath ragged bits of torn protective derma. Little blood was evident, though another clear liquid made a short but copious effusion from the insult, which I could only suspect to be spinal fluid. I winced, watching on along with the others: next Eamon's knife blade was sunk once vertically into exposed matter, to the hilt.

I'd thought the convict dead by then, but upon the knife's insertion, the prone body strained once very quickly, bowed upward, then flopped inert.

A long but subdued *Ahhhhhhhhhh . . .* , issued from the advertent watchers.

Eamon's eyes blazed now as the killer's had, but not with iniquity, with retribution; & it was these eyes that surveyed the circle of hushed onlookers. Then came a signal: a knowing nod. From the human rotary, only the male members detached themselves, to merge into a snakelike line behind Eamon at the (& do pardon the pun) the "head" of the table.

That premonitory "prickling" of my hands which had shadowed me all the day now overwhelmed my entire being such that I felt electrically charged. Because, you see, what followed can only be transliterated as silent, measured, purposeful, & very cumulative insanity.

I must select my words with care.

The comeliest of the women spectating from the circle (concurrently, mind you, as if automatonic) divorced themselves of their exiguous (& in some cases, almost non-existent) garb, to stand wild-eyed, sweating, & utterly naked in the firelight. This licentious display seized my attention all-inclusively as I suspect it would any natural man. Nipples jutting like plugs from young, heavy breasts; trim, enticing abdomens; toned, coltish legs; & abundantly furred pubises–these vivid & potent sights were what commandeered my gaze; I gulped at the virtual smorgasbord of visual rapture, & began to sweat profusely about the collar. But the figure my eyes were hottest for was that of the uniquely nubile albiness, & when she was found, my loins cringed in a dense, throat-parching, & sex-starved frisson. A concupiscent wraith she was, a shadow-land siren song, with her blanched & oddly shining skin & the head full of akink hair the color of anemic blood dusted by a whiteness that was pallid & lustrous simultaneously. Her body burgeoned as the ripest fruit. She eyed me again, an inviting leer, but stood poised as if her intention was to brazenly set her body out for showcase to the queue of men behind Eamon. I knew I was not in error when I noticed all said men scanning these nude enchantresses, their eyes asquint, their thoughts clearly fuming in ruttish intent. Was this to be some parachronistic Druid orgy, or a moon-lit fertility jubal as those slavering, totemistic rites which took place 5 millennia agone in the name of the Earth Mother? Could something so archaically bacchanalesque have somehow transplanted itself *here?*

No. This was something else altogether. Something more methodized, yet arcane & immemorially inhered nonetheless.

Something, too, my most ghastly nightmares could never have concocted.

At last, my will supervened the nagging lust in my heart, & I forced my eyes away from the sultry agglomeration of unclothed women, to look—

Gad, I can scarcely recount . . .

To look back at the head of the table.

What I saw is simpler to baldly state, & that was this: Eamon was copulating with the dead man's head.

Yes.

His work-pants ringed his ankles, his large hands pressed against the ears of the decedent, while his hips . . . *thrust* to & fro.

Hence, the function of the inscrutable knife-slit, to create a proper egress for the . . .

The act.

Horrific as this was, I pinpointed my vision on the area of (for lack of better terminology) *violation;* &, lo, too well I could see the glistening stem of Eamon's erection pistoning in & out of the convict's brain. Slowly, at first, then faster, harder. Each appalling stroke shot Eamon's eyes to a different woman, no doubt to sustain the necessary level of excitement for this ultimately *un*exciting task. Eamon's face began to strain, eyes puffing now, hips battering the crown of the convicts' head, faster, harder, frenetic. All that could be heard were the muted thumps of each buffeting impact of pelvis to head, & the synchronous wet *crinkle.*

It was then that someone said, "Hump it . . . "

Then a louder statement, "Hump it, Eamon!"

Another voice, louder still, "Git'cher dick up in there *deep,* brother!"

Next, a woman's voice, half-shrieking, "Fuck his brain ta puddin', Eamon!"

Then the loudest booming voice so far, that of the elder I'd glimpsed earlier: "EEEEEEEEEEEEEE-haaaa, Eamon! Hump that head, son! I say *HUMP* it!"

It was as though that trumpet-blast rebel vociferation had in some unknowable way unloosed total orgiastic endorsement. & hence forward?

Chaos.

As if by the snap of satanic fingers, I was standing numb & incomprehending, dead-center within an unknowable kaleidoscope of shrieking, throbbing, panting, ever-moving, copulative frenzy: pandemonium fit for the blackest arcades of Gehenna. All the men had either extracted their privates through their flies, released their trousers, or even stripped completely naked, churning, hips pumping in fornicative mimic, as they stroked themselves whilst leering at the mental sexual fodder, to wit: the young women void of garb with their paphian bodies & witch-fire eyes, so to sufficiently inflame their members for the hideous reward to come. The women themselves danced, writhed, & spun enfrenzied, desperately caressing one another's breasts, trading tongues, titillating the next's swollen nipples, or even more lewdly ranging their mouths from one bared pubis to the next; while one after another, the vengeance-crazed men—

There is no other way to relate it.

One after another (& as profanity is not my wont), they *fucked* the head of the dead man on that Tartarean table. I may even have drooled like a mad-house idiot, staring out, reminded at once of the horrid graffito I'd discovered in the garage commode-chamber. But this was no pervert-scrawl. This was real.

This was *taking place right now.*

Hellish images reflecting akin to flashes on a fiend's falling ax assaulted my eyes: tumid erections plunging into the raw brain like rods into a butter-churner, faces contorted in distilled animality, bodies stiffening & backs arched as if in burning torment yet lidless eyes showed an indubitable opposite; while crazed women danced, sprang, & twirled like an organic perpetual-motion engine, a delirious horde of delectable, voluptuous feminine flesh. & sounds, sounds, the sheer, cacophonic *rampage* of sounds: machine-gun chuckles; hoots, hollers, whistles, & even rabid howls; waves of climactic moans; hootenanny caterwauls & climactical squeals more beast-like than human; & voices, voices, voices, instilled to *madness* with satyriac lust; retaliatory appetency; incubic prurience & succubic guttle–the absolutely unnameable abandon which hit me as an omni-directional cannonade from ravening throats male & female alike as the spiriferous melee surged to incogitability:

68

"I'se a-comin', IIIIIIIIIIIIIIIIIIIII'se a-comin'!"

"Shee-IT, yeah! Thar's a great big dick-goober in the middle'a yer coconut!"

"Hump it, hump it, HUUUUUUUUUUUMP it!"

"How you lak that, fella? Huh? How you lak my big *dick* in yer head?"

"Fill 'im up, Deller! Fill that evil bastart's head with *cuuuuuuuuuuuuum!*"

"Yes sir! I'se comin' up a *storm* in this here killer's noggin! Ooooooooo-DOGGIE! He'll likely have my cum drippin' out his *ass!*"

"Git that nut, Tater! I say, *git* that nut!"

"Yeah! Squirt it way on up in 'nare!"

"Aw, jiminey, I'se got, I say I'se got so much jism pumpin' out my pecker it done feel like I'm takin' a blammed *piss,* it does!"

& from the hallucinotic outskirt of roaming, roving women, came a Cimmerian chant: "Fuck that head! Fuck that head! Fuck that-fuck that-FUCK that head!"

My soul smoldered as if I indeed slipped unknowingly into some insupposable byplace of the Hades. Even in the primevous, coruscating background, I could see some of the clan's boys–Clonner & Jake among them–half-hiding as they leered at the spectacle with pumpkin grins, masturbating energetically. Meanwhile, more adult clansmen had appeared & wasted no time stepping right up & draining the viscid merchandise of their loins into the killer's cranium like a player in a crap game all taking his turn. Other men whom I positively noticed to have already spent themselves had managed to refract & go again, a few even a *third time!* Then one very corpulent clodhopper sporting cauliflower ears, only a moment before a very vocal climax, withdrew his curiously arciformed erection from the unfortunate head, slapped the killer's face to one side, & ejaculated stout opalescent loops into the dead mouth. & just as the flickering, gaggling, moaning, shrieking, swaying, leaping, uncontemplatable mayhem finally would rise to such a pitch as to somehow spontaneously combust, the scene began to relent until it seemed to have run its frightful course, leaving the male participants standing stoop-shouldered or leaning against trees in exhaustion; or lying flat out on the ground, immobile from exertion, all limp-penised, cross-eyed, agape-mouthed; the women, too, sweat-gleaming as if varnished, their abundant chests heaving from fatigue, lay about entwined in one another like spent odalisques of some Plutonian harem. And as a final touch, in this macabre denouement, the aforementioned clan-elder approached the corpse on the table, tipped the head back over the edge, & marveled at the gush of semen that *poured* out, quite like milk from a filled-to-the-brim creamer. "Tarnations!" he cracked, "Would'ja *look*it all that nut we put in this som'bitch's head!"

I nearly collapsed in a faint.

Surely, I'd witnessed enough of "backwoods ways," even though a part of me *had* to shrive that this tenebrous mode of capital punishment made hanging, firing squad, & electrocution seem humdrum when juxtaposed. Ordinarily, I would never think of taking my leave of a host without bidding proper adieu (it would've been un-genteel) but under *these* circumstances?

It was time to leave, with *prompt* dispatch, I'd say.

I back-stepped, hoping to be indiscreet, slipped behind a flickering torch, & prepared to canter my way out of these forbidden woods, back to the road which would return me to Nate's ramshackle garage. I felt myself sinking into shadow, & in a moment had disappeared from the nefarious clearing. Still soul-shocked by what I'd descried, I stumbled away into darkness barely veined by moonlight filtering down through the limbs of the gnarled, serpentine trees overhead; & when I turned to bolt away–

"Howard!" came a hot, hushed whisper. "Ya can't up'n leave now! Ya just *cain't!*"

The sudden start may have momentarily halted my heart. At once, moist hands were on me, & then from the darkness, an earthy yet enticing, white figure emerged as of a sensualistic marble statue emerging from a pool of black ink: the preeminently figured woman I'd come to think of as the "albiness."

Once I realized who she was, I felt a hair-trigger surge in my libido; but all I had time to speak was, "Um, my, I . . . ," & that was all the situation permitted me to voice before the woman roughly embraced me, pressed her lips to mine, & plunged her tongue into my mouth. Her breasts, perfect to a preposterous degree, squashed against my chest like ethereal prods, charging me with a steaming, licentious heat; indeed, her nipples were so stoked by goatish desire, they could've been bolt-heads poking my shirt. Forthwith, I shot to tiptoes when an importunate hand kneaded my member through my trousers with the deftness of a practiced milk maid's on the teat of a cow. I tried to pull away–why, I was not sure at this point–but then other feminine hands–*many* of them–assailed my body & literally pulled me down onto the forest's carpet. Against my will, my shirt was opened; soft, wet lips lowering to lick my chest & draw in my own nipples. "Git his pants down!" someone commanded . . .

& it was so, posthaste.

"Howard," the albiness pleaded, "please don't leave us yet!"

I don't appear to have much of a CHOICE! I thought sarcastically, because I was being held down with dominance, hands pinning my arms to the ground, more hands following suit upon my legs, unyielding as iron fetters; & then my alarmed gaze roved an upward half-circle to see that at least a half-dozen "creeker" women–the very women who'd participated in the obscene ritual at the clearing, & all still shiningly naked–knelt about me, holding me fast to the ground as if I'd been *staked* there. Women, yes, the weaker sex, but these women were *hill* women, with bodies not only staggeringly provocative but bodies toned, conditioned, &, moreover, *strong* from the rigors of life in the hinterlands, far stronger–I hasten to add—than this spindly, lily-handed, 146-pound scribe. I may as well have had a pallet of grain sacks sitting atop me.

"See, see," the albiness panted, straddling me with her bare groin to my bare belly, "we just cain't have it–you leavin' without a-fuckin' us. You'se a hero! We need yer *seed,* Howard."

In the moonlight, I gaped up at her face, which was now flushed pink with excitement, as were her breasts & tops of her arms, while the rest of her remained the fascinating slick-white. Her nipples, now, stuck out surely as coat pegs. Eventually, I jabbered, "Mum-mum-my *seed?*"

"Aw, *shore,* baby!" she replied in a voice like warm, exotic fluid while mouths & tongues still laved my chest & more hands stroked my legs. "Ain't no one special *never* come through here—"

"I assure you, Miss, I'm hardly *special.* You should see my reviews—"

"—then all's a sudden *you* come along'n catch that devil's-dick-suckin' bag'a swamp scum that did that awful thang ta Sary. Howard, you'se the first hero we'se ever seen!"

This again! "Really, girls, you're very lovely; in fact, if there were one word I could deem accurate enough to be applied to the physical beauty of you all . . . it would be the word *superlative—*"

The crowd of faces peering down burst into chattery laughter.

"Hush, now, with yer fancified words," cooed the albiness. Her eyes seemed even to *glow* a startling red. "Just go on'n give us what we need. Cain't hardly *believe* ya wouldn't wanna."

Another face—hovering over magnificent breasts, mind you—urged forward into greater moonlight, & considered with concern, "Less'n yer one'a them *homo*-types, a *queer*-boy. Well, *is* ya?"

Even in the crush of this calamity, I frowned, "I assure you ladies, I most incontestably am of no such persuasion—"

"He's right!" another one, a huge-eyed—and huge-*bosomed*—blonde exclaimed.

Another, in a lovely, lilting voice: "Well, holy everlivin' *shit!*" & another pixie simply squealed in glee.

"Bleechy!" squealed another. "Git'cher ass off'a him so's we can *all* see!"

Back-lighted by a shaft of lunar light, the albiness—"Bleechy," I'd now been given notice—began to rise from her uncouth but not unpleasing straddle, the shifty moonlight turning her sprawl of kinky hair to a sex-spirit's orphic aura; & when she stepped aside–

The response of the remaining women couldn't have been more gleefully *mad*. Exclamations of the most shrill & giddy approval shot from every voluptuous mouth.

"Gawd, durn! It's huge!"

A whistle of giggles, then: "It looks like a shaved weasel, it does!"

"This hero-man shore got himself a *rig,* don't he?"

"That there's enough dang *meat* ta hang in a blammed smokehouse!"

I could not conceive as to their meaning, but then, another shrieked & blurted:

"Why, that's the biggest motherfuckin' *dick* I ever gandered in my *life!*"

Preposterous. Evidently they were referring to the dimensions of my genitals, though I'm quite certain they sported nothing especial in that department. They must only be saying such things to be polite to a visitor . . .

Now the albiness, Bleechy, stood over me, one bare foot to either side of my hips, her hands on her *own* hips, & she looked down red-eyed in the tinseled moonlight & in a manner purred like a feline. My eyes roved slowly upward, examining every perceptible detail of her luscious physique. She was an ivory tower of the most succulent, intoxicating woman-flesh. "Howard, you are, I say you are shorely somethin, you is. Like a breath'a fresh air come through this shit-hole. A hero–"

My eyes rolled. "Miss, in all seriousness, I'm *not* a h–"

"–and smart as a whip and all full'a big fancified city words–"

"I'll admit, I'm a bit bookish, have been since I was four. See, I was taught to read early, as well as possessing a connatural proclivity for reading–"

"–and *handsome–*"

Speechlessness struck me like lightning.

"–and mixed up with all that, *what'choo* got 'tween yer legs? A pecker bigger'n *any one ever been part'a this clan!*"

73

A gulp seized me. *Could this be true?* No! It was only graciousness that urged remarks of such kudos. Notwithstanding, I wasn't here to be complimented (nor *raped* by a bevy of young women *so attractive* they existed essentially as caricatures of feminine desire!) *Happenstance* had navigated me here, happenstance & only that. All that weighed on my mind–Bliss—had been relinquished to some subconscious repository during the distractive madness I'd just witnessed. *Bliss,* I thought forlornly. What was she suffering now? What was she thinking?

& here I was lying with my pants down & my genitals exposed before a rabble of naked "creeker" girls.

Never have I felt more ashamed.

"Ladies, I must *go!*" I asserted in my beefiest voice, & then I summoned all my strength to break the bond of so many hands holding me fast to the ground.

I didn't budge, & giggles burst like scattered night-birds.

"You ain't goin' *nowhere,* Howard," Bleechy's voice bubbled down. "If'n you ain't gonna give us yer business, we'se just gonna have ta take it . . . but what'cha gotta understart, hon, is we'se takin' it with enough thanks ta fill a blammed *pig-trough.*"

An . . . interesting manner with which to legitimize abduction, imprisonment, &, ostensibly, the forcible engagement of carnal knowledge upon an unwilling victim.

"Please understand, gentlewomen," I implored, "my conscience, if you must know, is bound to another woman. I'm sure I would not be able to . . . perform."

More chatterous laughter rose up like alien surf. A wide-hipped, plug-nippled, & quite mind-boggling brunet chuckled to object, pointing downward. "Not perform, huh? Then why's yer peckerwood hard as a fencepost & dang near as big?"

I could not contrive a response.

"One at a time, girls," ordered the albiness (pronunciating the word "time" as *tam*), then plopped her shapely groin down on my erection . . . & squealed. In pain-staking slowness, she rode my privates up & down. The sensation was, admittedly, quite pleasurable. "Don't'cha git'cher nut, baby. Just give us

74

each'a little sit-down first, okay?"

"I assure you, I do not receive your meaning!"

Her eyes rolled back in her head as one possessed by a daemonic entity, & the moan that escaped "Bleechy's" throat seemed unworldly. "Ah, oh, hon! Fuck–oh, Howard . . . Ain't never felt *nothin'* so's good as this!" Her hand quickly plied her own privates (baring a peach-seed-sized clitoris out, shiny & pale-pink) during the course of my penetration, when, with a chilling promptitude, she shrieked with all the force her lungs could conscript. Meanwhile, a darkly lovely face huddled close–it was one of the breast-heavy women who held my arms immobilely to the ground–and whispered, "See, Sir, we'se need ya ta give us all yer *nut.*"

My face must have corrugated with confusion. "Pardon me, but . . . my *nut?* If by that you mean my *semen,* then I'll point out the *impossibility* of one man trafficking his *sperm* to a dozen-plus women in a single foregathering!"

It was the sated Bleechy who now knelt beside me, patting my head as though I were a listless pet. "Just don't let'cherself come while each gal has a nice sit-down on yer prick–"

"*What?*" I raised my voice at the absurd inference.

"Just you think 'bout what fellas do when's they'se holdin' back, then leave the rest ta li'l ole me. See, I'se got a *system!*"

I had not an idea in the world of what she spoke; I could only assume she expected me to slake the loins of *all these women* . . . without ejaculating?

Bleechy continued, as now the 4th or 5th woman took her turn being impaled by me, "We'se need ya ta git'cher seed up in us, *all*'a us, so's some of us might get *pregnant* . . . "

"It's a *hero's* nut we all need up'n our cunnies," another preposterously chested girl explained, "a smart, handsome, *city*-man's nut!"

"—so's ta git some of us knocked up with a *hero's* baby!"

Oh, for the sake of Agamemnon!

It proceeded as thus: one stepped on, sat down, rode her hips manically until her crises was reached, then stepped off to make room for the next, & throughout I was forced to listen to the most shrill cries of satisfaction:

"Feels lak I'se got a *gopher* stuck up me!"

"This dick's twice as big as anythin' I been fucked by!"

"Uh! Uh! Uh! Uh! Uh . . . . Ahhhhhhhhhhhhhhhhh!"

"Oh, I'se just *swear* this hero-fella's peter is pushin' 'gainst my stomach!"

"Oooooooo, that there's just the best the best the best the best everlin' *fuckin'* I'se ever gots in my whole cotton-pickin' LIFE!"

& more of the same.

So aggravated was I by their misconception of–I cannot help it–conception, my mind felt quite divided from my undeniably aroused member, such that the annoyed distraction did indeed enable me to forestall orgasm, while the women continued to use my erection for a, so to speak, carnal "scratching-post." Bleechy kept patting my head as the waiting line, at long last, dwindled.

& when the last woman was finished?

"*Now,* Howard," gushed Bleechy, "*now* you'se can have yer nut," & she swivelled where she knelt, lowered her face, & pulled into her mouth the entirety of my sexual architecture. Instantly I clenched, my toes curling as if to break the souls out of my shoes. Through delectation-narrowed eyes, I managed to glance at the locale of the act, & saw Bleechy engaged in very methodical & adroit fellatio, her lips stretched painfully tight around the girth of my organ. It was rhythmic, machinelike, & rife with suction but the culmination she apparently wanted felt unsummonable: my mind was still at odds with sundries, & when I remembered my chief worry–Bliss–I felt, oddly, that I was being unfaithful to her, an absurd notion, I know; nonetheless, I was even less confident that I would be able to finalize the act to completion.

Bliss. What further horrors had O'Slaughnassey inflicted upon her since I'd departed? What lies might he be telling her about me? Did she now dismiss me as a coward?

These prospects injected me with a most dreadful anxiety, such that Bleechy could sense this by some, I suppose, "hill-tramp" intuition.

"Howard, honey? Ain't you likin' the feel'a my mouth on yer peter?"

"I . . ."

"Aw, you mean you'se're feelin' guilty 'bout that other gal you mentioned? Well, why nots just pretend it's *her* suckin' yer dick 'stead'a me!"

The suggestion sounded like so much nonsense–by now I was absolutely *disconsolate* via my fears for Bliss; yet some Freudian toggle seemed to click in my head with nearly an audible snap. Then:

It *was* Bliss I imagined fellating me, then crawling forward to be penetrated, & then, then–

Smiling resplendently, her eyes abeam with love for me, & her nearly inapprehensibly beautiful body shimmering, *then* she took my member in the "grip" of her deformed foot . . . & began to stroke.

This chimeral image alone, after only a moment, caused my loins to break like a veritable dam; & into the intricate webwork of my libidinal nerves was flooded ecstasy like that experienced by opium-smokers. I shuddered, stretched out & straining against the forest thatch beneath me, moaning outright; & with one spasm after the next, my seminal fluids were relocated into Bleechy's hot mouth. Evidently, said spasms did not abate when she expected them to, for soon (after, perhaps, the 12th or 15th spasm) the albiness's ruby-corundum eyes shot open in what could only be flabbergastment, & she actually released a muffled mewl. After 5 more spasms–well, perhaps 10–the dispensation was at an end; so, too, was my soul-upheaving orgasm. Winded in the literary "afterglow," I looked to Bleechy to express some exhausted gratitude & compliment her on such formidable skill, but by now she'd disengaged from my privates & knelt bug-eyed, a hand to her closed mouth.

"Gawd, dang," one of the other curvaceous sprites remarked. "Looks lak Bleechy got's herself a mouthful!"

Indeed, along with the expression of utter shock on her face, her cheeks ballooned; they appeared *stuffed* akin to the cheek-pouches of a foraging chipmunk. She made noises in her throat whose meaning I could not imagine, then turned & crawled aside.

Edward Lee

To whither is she crawling? I wondered.

On my left, I discerned that all of the promiscuettes who'd used my penis for a "sit down" were all lying prone in a line, lying, yes, with their legs lewdly spread, their hair-crowded pubises lewdly raised, & their fingers–lewdest of all–curled into the tender vulvic entries in order to deliberately open them.

Of all the falderal!

One needn't have earned dual doctorates in predicate calculus & existential thaumaturgology to now discern the full meaning of Bleechy's "system . . . "

Up to the crotch of each spread-legged nymph Bleechy nuzzled; for lack of more eloquent metaphor, she then "fish-lipped" her mouth & daintily expectorated a small allotment of my semen from the reservoir of her mouth into each opened orifice, which I suppose might suffice as a mode of fertilisation. Each woman giggled upon "receipt." Bleechy spat the last of it into her own hand &, amongst slick, indelicate sounds, rubbed it into her own sex, pushing her fingers deep, all the while peering at me in astonishment: "Well, holy jumpin' jiminy, Howard! Not only've ya got a giant dick, ya done *cum* more'n a blammed Appaloosa stallion!"

As I pulled up my trousers, my brow creased like an accordion, as I wanted to ask how Bleechy in the first place *knew* how much "cum" said equus might produce, but then . . .

I thought the better of it.

The girls began to disband, all hailing some mode of farewell, to wit: "'Bye, Mister hero!" & "If'n I git knocked up, I'll'se name my baby *Howard!*" & "Oh, I just knows I'm gonna have me a baby now–a *hero*-baby!" & "G'night, Mister! Thanks fer yer nut!"

I groaned wearisomely. Would any of them actually become impregnated? Would *many* of them?

With my luck, I suspected, *they all will . . .*

I watched, still stupefied, as they disappeared like salacious eidolons amid the twisted trees and dapples of moonlight.

Bleechy was all who remained. "Thank ya so much, Howard," & she leaned & kissed me. I couldn't have

78

grimaced more intensely, as her tongue ploughing into mine no doubt was still rife with the presence of my own sperm (or, to use a previous fine gentleman's kingly lexicon, my own "dick-goober.") Then she winked & gave my crotch 2 quick squeezes, like the rubber bulb on a child's bicycle horn. "You really are quite a man!" I might point out that she pronounced the word "quite" as *qwatt.*

When she'd made her exit, I wiped my mouth off on my arm–*yuck!*— &, feeling a perfect lackwit, struggled to drag myself up; half-way through the effort, however, a big hand grabbed my wrist &—

"There ya go, Howard!"

The shadowed hulk before me was Eamon, far less tense than he'd been, evidently, since partaking in his relief. As though my body lacked mass altogether, he lifted me to my feet.

"Thank you, Eamon."

"It's we'se who's thankin' you, Sir. Fer all ya done," the great, rough voice issued. He glanced aside, where the last of the nude women disappeared–then he smiled. "Aw, I see Bleechy'n her gals just showed ya some southern harspitality." He elbowed me with a wink. "Bet they filched yer cum, huh?"

Drawn & haggard, all I could say was, "Um, uh . . . yes. They did indeed."

Eamon emitted a hearty chuckle. "Them gals're sumpthin, yesiree. They pult that stunt on some fella couple'a years ago, fed'ral man, some guy from state wildlife department're some such; & I'll be danged if five of 'em didn't get preggered by his nut." His big hand cracked me on the back. "Howard, I just want'cha ta know we'se'll be plumb honored ta have some'a yer hero's blood runnin' in our clan . . . "

I wobbled in place at the data.

"But on ta more serious stuff–thank ya from the bottom'a my heart fer what'cha done. Catchin' that devil the way ya did, and allowin' us to see ta proper punishment . . . why, now me'n my whole clan, we'se can sleep in peace. Just want'cha ta know how's grateful we is."

"Yuh-yuh-yuh . . . you're quite welcome," I absurdly

replied, knowing I must now disengage. "It's time for me to be off, though–I've an early bus."

"'A'course, a'course!" boomed the big voice. "I reckon what'cha seen here weren't quite what'cha 'spected, but ya gots ta remember, we'se from different worlds."

I nodded, exhausted. "And from different worlds, Eamon, different ways . . . . *Backwoods* ways, in this instance . . . "

His eyes bored into me. "That's a-right, Howard. Ya truly are a hero, and I'm shore proud as *shit* my two boys got ta be in yer presence. But before ya leave, is there anythin' I'se can do fer ya?"

I was about to answer a hasty *no*, but then that esoteric fugue returned to the backdrop of my mind &, hence, my spirit . . .

2 May, 19—
daybreak

The horizon's creeping acclivity in the east flamed with the molten colours of dawn when my feet made the last steps toward my destination. A smile in my eye, I spied the dilapidated wooden sign mounted on the ramshackle building: NATE'S GAS & REPAIRS. *Finally*... Fatigue & a more than understandable shock had hindered my ordinarily brisk pace of walking. The chirping frolic of birds seemed to greet me as I approached the dingy garage–at once I felt energized in spite of my tiredness; & it was with a sudden spring in my step that I ambulated on. In a distant lot, the bus (with a hatch opened in the back, & one who could only be Nate leaning into it) was next to snag my gaze; i.e., the repairs were underway. Also, I noticed with some heartenment that those passengers who'd last evening opted for the nearby motel were returning as well.

I'd had enough of this place, & now was the time for me to be gone from it.

Inside the front "office" I was immediately alarmed to find the British slatternette was just coming awake upon the tattered couch, dark hair disarranged. She rubbed sleep from her eyes, squinting. "Oh, it's you," her accent appraised.

"Good morn–" I began, then felt a start like a hard shove in the chest.

Where last time I'd seen this sordid-mouthed, busty tart, she'd been fit to erupt from late-term pregnancy, she now displayed no such evidence at all. As she groggily swivelled around on the couch, in fact, her abdomen appeared lithely slim beneath the burgeoning, un-brassiered breasts.

"Miss! No doubt, you've—"

She smiled just as a high-pitched squalling resounded from a back room; then a door clicked open.

Into the cramped office walked the 3 Floridian brothers,

81

all grinning proud as fathers themselves while in the arms of the central man churned a chubby newborn swaddled in linens. It bawled loud as an entire maternity ward (squalling babies have always irritated me) yet when one of the whiskery brothers tickled the infant's chin, it ceased its cacophony & giggled in oblivious glee.

"I dropped the li'l mate last night," came the mother's cockney explanation. "He's half-Yank, so I'm touchin' wood that's a smart mix."

A much more coarse accent—ugh, another *southern* accent—suffixed the new mother's words: the brother to the left. "See, me'n my brothers was thinkin', shit, we'se got ourselfs a big ole shack down Penser-kola, plennie'a room, and she ain't got nowhere's ta go, so . . . fuck! We'se invited her to come live with us, help her raise this li'l booger. It'll be like alls three'a us is the crumb-snatcher's father!"

I looked back in utter perplexion, while at the same time feeling quite guilty about having misjudged these men, dismissing them as simple yokels via their scruff appearance & ruffian deportment. "Why, what a noble and high-character gesture. You men surely are due serious praise to take on such a responsibility out of the charity of your hearts."

"Yeah!" said the middle brother. "It'll be the kind'a change we need, 'stead'a the same ole thang, just fishin' and drinkin'." (Aside, I'll point out that he pronounced "drinkin'" as *drankin'*) "Gawd knows she kin use a hand, specially the way the 'conomy is these days. It'll do us all good."

The 3rd one, grinning, leaned over close, & whispered with a snigger, "'Sides, as fine a fuck as *she* is, this limey tramp'll have us full *up* with pussy fer long as we want!"

Indeed.

But this knowledge was a bit of positivity I needed. A beam of unexpected light in a decidedly dark world. It was refreshing to perceive, and dampened my typically nihilistic impression of every one & every thing. Meanwhile, the baby *goo-goo*'d & *gaa-gaa*'d ad nauseam, but when the minuscule eyes within the pudgy face found their way to the mother's prodigious bosom, it began to squall again, to the extent that I ground my teeth.

"Alls it takes is one gander at momma's big-ass tits, and he up'n goes ape-shit," a brother said.

"Give 'im 'ere, love," said the woman, outstretching her arms. "He's 'ungry."

"He just *done* sucked a quart out that milk-cart."

"'E's a growin' boy!"

The central brother relinquished the infant; whereupon she uninhibitedly bared a breast. Without urging, the baby's tiny mouth immediately sought the distended nipple and began to suck.

"That's my lad!"

"Kid'll be tit-feedin' till he's twennie!" one brother roared, and the others cackled like daemonic parrots. I used the uproar's distraction to slip back out, unnoticed; nodding curtly to those others returning from the flagrantly-priced motel.

"Well, hail!" another voice shot loud enough to send a jolt from my shoes to my head, and then came an unprepared-for slap upon my back.

This gesture was something I did *not* appreciate.

"Was *wonderin'* where ya gots yerself off too," informed Nate the mechanic. "When me'n the other fella was done sloppin' us up some carnie whores, we done looked all over fer ya, but—"

"Yes. I grew so engaged within the intricacies of the show, I'm afraid I was a bit late in attempting to locate you and the bus driver," said I. "I apologise for causing you any undue concern."

"Aw, ain't no big deal. Figgered a smart fella like you'd figger some way ta git back. But I'se glad ya didn't take much longer—"

"Pardon me?"

"Yer blammed bus is fixed. Didn't take me but a hour ta do the job."

"Why, that's delightful news! I commend you on your promptitude and expertise, and I thank you. Don't misread me, Sir. It is not that your . . . 'neck of the woods' has not enlivened me splendidly, but . . . I'm anxious to re-commence with my travels."

"Oh, shore ya are. But it weren't a total waste fer ya, huh?" He winked. "Ya got's to go to the carnival!"

"Yes," I all but croaked, feigning a smile.

He chuckled and–for *pity's* sake—rubbed his crotch. "Me'n that other fella? Ooo-ee! We'se *busted* some poon, we did. My peter kicked out so much joy juice last night"–and, yes, he pronounced "night" as *nat*–"likely as not I'll'se be plumb empty fer a week!"

"That's-that's . . . quite . . . "

"Don't know 'bout that driver fella, but I'se definite got me a triple."

"A *triple?* Isn't that . . . baseball terminology?"

He guffawed in wheezes. "Naw, fella! Far as whorin' goes, a triple's when ya spunk one in the hair-box, 'nother one in the can, and a third in the breadbasket."

I paled. "Ah. I see."

But a sudden concerned expression overcame the seedy man's countenance. "Aw, dang, I'se up'n fergot. Just a hour ago–'fore you got back–two men from the blammed county *sheriff's* department come by!"

"You . . . you don't say," I replied, stiffening a bit.

"Kid ya not, Slim. Drop by here while's it's still dark, lookin' all serious'n all." He curled his finger at me, and accentuated his expression in an attitude indicating the need for discernment. "They up'n tolt me there was a *murder* last night–"

The word brought a stall to my heart. "A mur–"

"Shhh! Best ta not let the others hear–don't want 'em bad-mouthin' the town. But I ain't lyin', not long after me'n the other fella git back, these county men bang on the door'n question us!"

"Qwuh-question, you say?"

"Yee-ip. Real serious-like." He lowered his whisper further, to near inaudibility. "See, sometime after the carnival close up? Some-'un dang snuck into the trailer'a O'Slaughnassey hisself! And up'n *kilt* him!"

"O'Slaughn–oh, you mean–"

Nate nodded as if a preceptor of vast wisdom; he pointed to the advert poster, to the proprietor's name. "The same dang guy who owns the *whole shebang,* yessir! Got kilt *bad,* too!" In counterfeit shock, I replied as I perceived anyone would. "That's terrible, certainly. But when you say the poor man was killed in a bad way . . . just . . . how do you mean?"

His shoulders popped in a quick shrug. "The coppers never tolt. But more'n a tad sick ta their bellies the both of 'em looked, I'll tell ya."

I cleared my throat. "What, um, what did they ask?"

He rolled a cigarette expertly with one hand. "Aw, just if we'd been, so we tolt 'em yeah—"

"Ah, so you apprised them that the three of us had attended the carnival, thanks to the free tickets offered by the tall man, yes?"

"Yee–er, no, now's that ya made me think of it. Plumb fergot to mention you went with us too. But after that they wanna know if'n we saw anyone suss-pisher-iss, like that. A'course, we didn't." His brow rose. "Did you?"

I cleared my throat again. "Why, no, I can't say that I did."

"World's all buggered up, ain't it? Killers, raperists, thieves–ever-where you look. Ain't no better in Warshingtin, ya ask me. Them fat cats is all lyin' like rugs'n gettin' rich whiles the rest'a us work our tookuses off for less'n ever if'n we'se even *got* a blammed job."

"I couldn't agree more," I said, a bit more cheerily than before. "But, my, what a regrettable tragedy. That poor man, Mr. O'Slaughnassey."

His expression, now, seemed to slough off my invented sentiment. "Aw, I wouldn't go mournin' *him*"–and then he *clapped* his hands abruptly in a way that not only annoyed me intensely but also signaled that his memory had just rekindled with a detail. "Dang fergot ta mention! 'Member that one whore I'se was harpin' 'bout last night? The blondie with no teeth'n hands fer feet who can suck dick like nobody's business'n jacks fellas off with her *feet*—"

"Yes, yes, I do recall, " I hastened, trying not to visibly wince; then pointed to the small, bawdy illustration on the poster. "Bliss, no doubt this woman right here."

"Yee-ip! I'se looked high'n low fer a dick-suck from *her,* but danged if'n she weren't even *workin'* last night. Was some big Irish lummox tolt me–"

Fortunately no bruises administered by the brute he referred to showed, and the few cuts and scrapes turned out to be of no consequence. The ache, however, in directions southerly of my belt were another tale . . .

"Anyway!" Nate went on, animated about something, "that same big-tit, young blondie whore Bliss–turns out that O'Slaughnassey was *her husband!*"

"That's beyond comprehension!" I maintained the pretense of alarm. "Her husband, you say?"

He cupped a hand to his mouth. "And her father, too!"

"No!"

"Yee-ip. Like I were saying, a buggered up world, an' chock full up with buggered up people, 'specially that O'Slaughnassey who ain't no better'n a dog. Any man'd marry his own daughter'n trick her out fer cash . . . well, that's the kind'a fella better off in the ground, ya ask me."

"My sentiments precisely," I offered, but it would've seemed odd not to ask the expected question. "So is Bliss a suspect, as one might presume?"

"Naw, not accordin' ta the cops. Said she fall down're somethin'n hurt herself so's she was in the carny doc's tent whiles O'Slaughnassey were gettin' his ticket punched."

"Ah. Probably random, then, theft-related."

"Likely as not. O'Slaughnassey was pig-shit rich from that show'n he's been doin' it fer decades, they said. 'Least, there's some good news, though."

"Really?"

"Good news fer the girl, I'se mean. See, her bein' married ta the scum, and him dyin', well, they said she'll inherit all his money'n the whole blammed carnival ta boot." He chuckled again. "I guess that there's what'cha call a *happy endin'*, huh?"

This I of course already knew, yet I play-acted a look of satisfaction. "Yes, yes, indeed, it is." I smiled. "A happy ending . . . "

He *snapped* his fingers in a sudden disgruntlement. "Just wish I could'a gotten me one'a them toothless cock-sucks off her. Ain't no way she'll be turnin' no tricks no more, that's fer shore, not with all'a O'Slaughnassey's loot."

"Mmm, you've a pertinent point. It's the young lady's good fortune, and I have the notion that she deserves it."

As the sun rose further, dragging a curtain of stunning, prismatic light across the fields, then the garage itself, Nate glanced at his watch in an after-thought. "Now where the *hail's* that dang driver? Must still be snoozin'. I'll shag his ass up'n let him know his bus is fixed."

"I'm sure he'll be very grateful, as are we all."

This proved the last of my discourse with the vulgarian mechanic whose final persuasions indicated at least some modicum of benevolence I hadn't otherwise detected. From this point, all was well, and details as to our sequent debarkation (which would, I'm happy to add, continue on toward my destinational goal: the sultry, atmosphere-rich city of New Orleans) needn't be expounded upon.

How the imponderably evil O'Slaughnassey came to meet his demise needn't be expounded upon, either, I shouldn't think. However, I will say that–on the evening prior—just before taking my leave of the baleful woodland clearing & the immense presence of one Eamon Martin, a few further words might be appreciated. I shall briefly recount:

Eamon had made a parting query, "But before ya leave, is there anythin' I'se can do fer ya?" I'd instinctively prepared to say "no" & be on my way. Simultaneously, however, my mind was abuzz with turmoil, founded chiefly by my own sense of regret & self-condemnation. What I regretted I would expect to be obvious: my failure to aid Bliss in her unspeakable travails. Earlier, I chatted with Eamon about the subjectivities of *justice;* I'd even proposed the certain legitimacy of effecting common-sense judicial license when crimes are committed outside the curtilege of established laws & also beyond the reach of police. " . . . proper engagement of the law where there *are* no formal laws," was something I'd said, if I recall with any accuracy. Though I can't say I approved of the manner with which the child-rapist/murderer had come to meet his decease, I must say I agreed with the end result: justice.

Eamon & his unkempt & uncultivated hillfolk had suffered a horror from which they could not turn a cheek; & hence were determined to do something about it, even though what they did was not within the letter of the law. It was that primitively simple.

Yes. These men would not rest until justice had been implemented. They *did* something about it.

But with regards to Bliss? I'd done *nothing*. I'd presumed instead to return to the dismal garage having aided Bliss not in the least, making every excuse in my coward's perceptions. That is why when Eamon had asked if there were anything he could do for me?

I'd steeled myself & answered, "Yes. I'd be grateful if you would be so generous as to give me a mallet similar to the one you made use of not too long ago . . . "

There was great risk, certainly, in returning to the carnival, but I believe that fortune was with me now, for absolutely no one who'd espied me on my first visit saw me upon this return. The mallet concealed in a bag, I played the part of an intrigued carnival-enthusiast until I'd quite stealthily re-found the execrable trailer where I knew O'Slaughnassey to abode. No component of scholarship nor deductive sleight is required to enlighten one of what followed. I shan't mention it again.

As for Bliss, I decided it best to never return to see her, as much as my heart yearned to. Her condition had no choice but to improve exponentially. What purpose might therefore be served by another meeting with her? She was young, beautiful, &, now, financially solvent for life. Never again would she be forced to engage in "tricks" or that heinous "peep-tent" act. She was the magnate of the travelling show now, & I'm confident she would serve it well, & vice-versa. In her new life, there'd be no comfortable place for a bookish, pining, reclusive man such as myself. For me, the memory of her smile, of the genuine look in her eyes, & of her kiss, was all I needed, & far more than I deserved.

Like the ruffian mechanic Nate has so said–a "happy

endin'."

Writers keep journals in order to attend to a variety of needs, i.e., the most likely for a majority is the simple "exercise" of craft. Others keep them to leave a personal record for descendants (hardly the case for me), while others (writers of a more self-aggrandized bent), to be published posthumously, to follow on in their fame (I can hardly count upon that!) For me, however, journaling provides an arcane & very effective catharsis. Had I not scribbled down this account before my eyes, I suspect I'd exist in quite a forlorn & intractable emotional status; but now that I've filtered the events through my mind & released them through my pen, I am able to come to terms with it all, & have managed to glean crucial & previously unrealised aspects of myself–I should say my deepest *inner* self. In spite of the truly unutterable horrors I'd witnessed, I am now more at peace than I have ever been, & better armed & opportuned to function within the world & proceed with my life. Odd as it may seem, I feel as though I've been blessed . . .

This entire matter is moot, however. Often I compose journals—I'm sure due to inclination & indoctrination—as though they are to be looked upon by typical readers. I've written many, many travel journals, for instance—& perhaps some of those shall be read by close friends &/or my literary executor after my demise. But that must not be the case in regard to this *particular* journal, wouldn't you agree? There are indeed potential legal ramifications, given my conduct of last evening. My full name does not appear here, & only one of a rare distilled fanaticism might identify me based on certain remarks herein. Unlikely, in other words. &, as an added good fortune, the Burlington Superior Bus Lines Co. does *not* require positive identification in order to purchase a ticket. Hence?

The proverb "Scot free" comes to mind.

I see that this particular coach is conveniently equipped with a waste receptacle by the exit door. The transfer point for my next connexion will soon be arrived at; therefore I've decided to tear these damnable sheets from my binder right

now, & then make prompt use of said receptacle upon my off-
boarding–

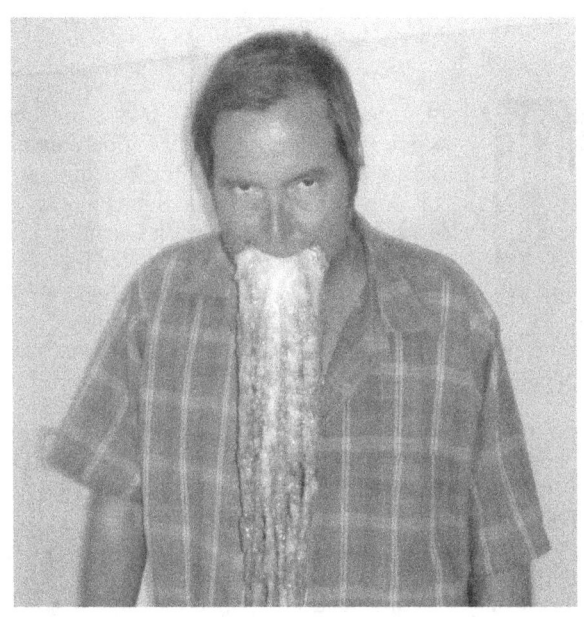

ABOUT THE AUTHOR

Edward Lee has authored close to 50 books in the field of horror; he specializes in hardcore fare. His most recent novels are LUCIFER'S LOTTERY and the Lovecraftian THE HAUNTER OF THE THRESHOLD. His movie HEADER was released on DVD by Synapse Film in June, 2009. Lee lives in Largo, Florida.

deadite press

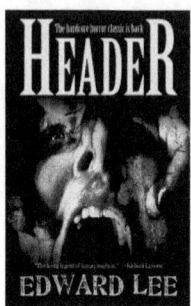

"Header" Edward Lee - In the dark backwoods, where law enforcement doesn't dare tread, there exists a special type of revenge. Something so awful that it is only whispered about. Something so terrible that few believe it is real. Stewart Cummings is a government agent whose life is going to Hell. His wife is ill and to pay for her medication he turns to bootlegging. But things will get much worse when bodies begin showing up in his sleepy small town. Victims of an act known only as "a Header."

"Red Sky" Nate Southard - When a bank job goes horrifically wrong, career criminal Danny Black leads his crew from El Paso into the deserts of New Mexico in a desperate bid for escape. Danny soon finds himself with no choice but to hole up in an abandoned factory, the former home of Red Sky Manufacturing. Danny and his crew aren't the only living things in Red Sky, though. Something waits in the abandoned factory's shadows, something horrible and violent. Something hungry. And when the sun drops, it will feast.

"Zombies and Shit" Carlton Mellick III - Twenty people wake to find themselves in a boarded-up building in the middle of the zombie wasteland. They soon discover they have been chosen as contestants on a popular reality show called Zombie Survival. Each contestant is given a backpack of supplies and a unique weapon. Their goal: be the first to make it through the zombie-plagued city to the pick-up zone alive. But because there's only one seat available on the helicopter, the contestants not only have to fight against the hordes of the living dead, they must also fight each other.

"Muerte Con Carne" Shane McKenzie - Human flesh tacos, hardcore wrestling, and angry cannibal Mexicans, Welcome to the Border! Felix and Marta came to Mexico to film a documentary on illegal immigration. When Marta suddenly goes missing, Felix must find his lost love in the small border town. A dangerous place housing corrupt cops, borderline maniacs, and something much more worse than drug gangs, something to do with a strange Mexican food cart...

deadite press

"Earthworm Gods" Brian Keene - One day, it starts raining-and never stops. Global super-storms decimate the planet, eradicating most of mankind. Pockets of survivors gather on mountaintops, watching as the waters climb higher and higher. But as the tides rise, something else is rising, too. Now, in the midst of an ecological nightmare, the remnants of humanity face a new menace, in a battle that stretches from the rooftops of submerged cities to the mountaintop islands jutting from the sea. The old gods are dead. Now is the time of the Earthworm Gods...

"Earworm Gods: Selected Scenes from the End of the World" Brian Keene - a collection of short stories set in the world of Earthworm Gods and Earthworm Gods II: Deluge. From the first drop of rain to humanity's last waterlogged stand, these tales chronicle the fall of man against a horrifying, unstoppable evil. And as the waters rise over the United States, the United Kingdom, Australia, New Zealand, and elsewhere-brand new monsters surface-along with some familiar old favorites, to wreak havoc on an already devastated mankind..

"An Occurrence in Crazy Bear Valley" Brian Keene- The Old West has never been weirder or wilder than it has in the hands of master horror writer Brian Keene. Morgan and his gang are on the run--from their pasts and from the posse riding hot on their heels, intent on seeing them hang. But when they take refuge in Crazy Bear Valley, their flight becomes a siege as they find themselves battling a legendary race of monstrous, bloodthirsty beings. Now, Morgan and his gang aren't worried about hanging. They just want to live to see the dawn.

"Entombed II" Brian Keene- It has been several months since the disease known as Hamelin's Revenge decimated the world. Civilization has collapsed and the dead far outnumber the living. The survivors seek refuge from the roaming zombie hordes, but one-by-one, those shelters are falling. Twenty-five survivors barricade themselves inside a former military bunker buried deep beneath a luxury hotel. They are safe from the zombies...but are they safe from one another?

"Urban Gothic" Brian Keene - When their car broke down in a dangerous inner-city neighborhood, Kerri and her friends thought they would find shelter inside an old, dark row home. They thought they would be safe there until help arrived. They were wrong. The residents who live down in the cellar and the tunnels beneath the city are far more dangerous than the streets outside, and they have a very special way of dealing with trespassers. Trapped in a world of darkness, populated by obscene abominations, they will have to fight back if they ever want to see the sun again.

"Ghoul" Brian Keene - There is something in the local cemetery that comes out at night. Something that is unearthing corpses and killing people. It's the summer of 1984 and Timmy and his friends are looking forward to no school, comic books, and adventure. But instead they will be fighting for their lives. The ghoul has smelled their blood and it is after them. But that's not the only monster they will face this summer . . . From award-winning horror master Brian Keene comes a novel of monsters, murder, and the loss of innocence.

"Clickers" J. F. Gonzalez and Mark Williams- They are the Clickers, giant venomous blood-thirsty crabs from the depths of the sea. The only warning to their rampage of dismemberment and death is the terrible clicking of their claws. But these monsters aren't merely here to ravage and pillage. They are being driven onto land by fear. Something is hunting the Clickers. Something ancient and without mercy. *Clickers* is J. F. Gonzalez and Mark Williams' gore-soaked cult classic tribute to the giant monster B-movies of yesteryear.

"Clickers II" J. F. Gonzalez and Brian Keene- Thousands of Clickers swarm across the entire nation and march inland, slaughtering anyone and anything they come across. But this time the Clickers aren't blindly rushing onto land - they are being led by an intelligence older than civilization itself. A force that wants to take dry land away from the mammals. Those left alive soon realize that they must do everything and anything they can to protect humanity – no matter the cost. *This isn't war, this is extermination.*

AVAILABLE FROM AMAZON.COM

deadite press

"Dark Hollow" Brian Keene - Eerie, piping music is heard late at night, and mysterious fires have been spotted deep in the woods. Women are vanishing without a trace overnight, leaving behind husbands and families. When up-and-coming novelist Adam Senft stumbles upon an unearthly scene, it plunges him and the entire town into an ancient nightmare. Folks say the woods in LeHorn's Hollow are haunted, but what waits there is far worse than any ghost. It has been summoned…and now it demands to be satisfied.

"The Cage" Brian Keene - For the employees of Big Bill's Home Electronics, it's just the end of another long workday—until a gunman bursts into the store and begins shooting. Now, with some of their co-workers dead, the hostages are disappearing one-by-one, and if they want to survive the night, they'll have to escape… THE CAGE.

"Castaways" Brian Keene- They came to the deserted island to compete on a popular reality television show. Each one hoped to be the last to leave. Now they're just hoping to stay alive, because the island isn't deserted after all. Contestants are disappearing, but they aren't being eliminated by the game. They're being taken by the monstrous, half-human creatures that live deep in the jungle. The men will be slaughtered. The women will be kept alive as captives. Night is falling, the creatures are coming, and rescue is so far away…

"Kill Whitey" Brian Keene- In the Russian criminal underworld there is a man named Whitey. He is unstoppable and always gets what he wants. Some say he can't be hurt. Some say he can't be killed. Larry Gidson is about to find out. He is a dock worker on the run with Sondra Belov, a beautiful stripper. Whitey wants Sondra and he will torture and kill to get her. Larry, his friends, and even his cat will never be safe unless they give him Sondra – or they kill Whitey.

"A Gathering of Crows" Brian Keene - Five mysterious figures are about to pay a visit to Brinkley Springs. They have existed for centuries, emerging from the shadows only to destroy. To kill. To feed. They bring terror and carnage, and leave blood and death in their wake. The only person that can prevent their rampage is ex-Amish magus Levi Stoltzfus. As the night wears on, Brinkley Springs will be quiet no longer. Screams will break the silence. But when the sun rises again, will there be anyone left alive to hear?

"Take the Long Way Home" Brian Keene - All across the world, people suddenly vanish in the blink of an eye. Gone. Steve, Charlie and Frank were just trying to get home when it happened. Trapped in the ultimate traffic jam, they watch as civilization collapses, claiming the souls of those around them. God has called his faithful home, but the invitations for Steve, Charlie and Frank got lost. Now they must set off on foot through a nightmarish post-apocalyptic landscape in search of answers. In search of God. In search of their loved ones. And in search of home.

"Darkness on the Edge of Town" Brian Keene - One morning the residents of Walden, Virginia, woke up to find the rest of the world gone. Surrounding their town was a wall of inky darkness, plummeting Walden into permanent night. Nothing can get in - not light, not people, not even electricity, radio, TV, internet, food, or water. And nothing can get out. No one who dared to penetrate the mysterious barrier has ever been seen again. But for some, the darkness is not the worst of their fears.

"Tequila's Sunrise" Brian Keene - Discover the secret origins of the "drink of the gods" in this dark fantasy fable by best-selling author Brian Keene. Chalco, a young Aztec boy, feels helpless as conquering Spanish forces near his village. But when a messenger of the gods hands him a key to unlock the doors of human perception and visit unseen worlds, Chalco journeys into the mystical Labyrinth, searching for a way to defeat the invaders. He will face gods, devils, and things that are neither. But he will also learn that some doorways should never be opened and not all entrances have exits... Tequila's Sunrise.

THE VERY BEST IN CULT HORROR